Photo by Brenda Burdick

Dedication

I dedicate this book to my grandchildren, who I encourage to read endlessly and write each day as a habit.

Brianna Sancious
Myles Sancious
Victor Roldan
Maya Roldan
Walker Burdick
Cooper Burdick

West To Big Water

A Civil War Aftermath

By Garry Camp Burdick

WEST TO BIG WATER

Design and Layout by Kim Burdick
Cover photo by Brenda Burdick

iUniverse books may be ordered through booksellers or by contacting:

iUniverse
1663 Liberty Drive
Bloomington, IN 47403
www.iuniverse.com
1-800-Authors (1-800-288-4677)

ISBN: 978-1-4620-3638-7 (sc)
ISBN: 978-1-4620-3639-4 (ebk)

Printed in the United States of America

iUniverse rev. date: 07/12/2011

Table of Contents

Poetry

Wind and a Poet

A solid wind driving up from bay waters lifted Garth's body into the deep white of the non-transparent cloud sheathing his form, allowing him the disguise to ascend into his own space above the work party below. Garth ignored the warning of attempting to climb beyond his assigned work near the top of the unfinished tower of the San Francisco bridge. He leaned into the winds energy with no fear in his heart. Garth, the grandson of Target, had disclosed within his poetry of his wish to fly as a sea gull floating on the currents of cool air vaulting off the big water of the pacific. He likened himself to the freedom of both wind and flight, the year was 1937.

Moments before, the wind had shifted direction, bemused with the magnificent space he was occupying within the lingering fog his body left it's perch as though lifted by a hand above. He had stood for weeks hoping to be called forth from the crowd, wanting work of any type on this magnificent bridge. Jobs were few and far between during this long depression.

This newly hired, inexperienced bridge laborer appeared to glide outward and forward with the up draft blowing from under the tower. This moment of perpendicular flight had Garth in it's power and he felt as though he were in control gliding over the bay like an giant Condor. He wished his father could see him now. His direction was due West out toward the open Ocean, he felt he was in command of this flight. His mind placed his grandfather's image beside his flight motioning with his good arm to come this way, closer, pointing westward.

Garth's cramped garrett at the forth floor of a home on Pacific Heights was filled with his papers, each holding words of adventures, loves, limited travel, and above all his poems that now and again appeared in a San Francisco free press. Also a pocket-sized published volume of many of his poems which had offered him some small celebrity among established poetry groups in town. He spent time each day looking out of a half moon shaped window, watching the wind in the canvas sails of ships, the sun sets, the fog, moved by all this beauty he needed to write on paper the fabric of what he sensed.

The time of Garth's flight was brief and filled with pictures of his short life, his mother, his school days, his growing up as the mulatto child of a black civil war veteran and a white Chickasaw woman from Oregon. Above the rushing air he heard his father say that this was his destiny, to labor on the connecting of north and south, a "Golden Gate", he pronounced. Garth fell earthward into the big water of the San Francisco Bay. His body thou searched for was never found, however a jacket he left hanging in the workers shack near the bottom of the bridge tower was discovered, his address written on the inside cover of his published poetry book.

An acquaintance, by the name of Christopher who had gained work the month before and had coached Garth on just where to situate himself to be chosen from the assembly of men looking for work, was the one to find the coat and poetry book and went to the address to explain to Garth's landlady the tragic disappearance. She at once, without ceremony, or sympathy, offered him the rent and he took possession of it without seeing it's size or contents.

Garth's room was small harboring an ambience beyond anything that Chris had ever witnessed. His life had been filled with nothing but tent living or cheap hotels where men slept three in a bed. Here he found images on the walls, far off places, hand colored art work, that seemed so life like to Chris that he believed he couldn't touch them. The bed was made, the desk was neat, the shelves held books perfectly aligned and well worn from their many readings. He gazed out the half moon window, the tower of the bridge where Garth had slipped was clearly in view.

On the desk was a leather bound booklet a title written in bold black ink read, "West To Big Water by George Washington Target. Chris embarked into it's narrative.

2

Saddle up

*"The following words will attempt to tell of myself and two ex
Union soldiers who rode from east to west with me. A journey with
my leaving Virginia, and they departing Connecticut. Though
the friendships were forged during the war between the states,
the events of my story begin at the horse farm of Garry Sherman
Camp in New Milford , CT."*

The September air brilliant with the beech nut fragrance offered
by leaves gliding toward earth like giant red and yellow moths. A
New England autumn, several years after the defeat and surren-
der of the South by General Lee to General Grant the time - still within
the healing hours of a fight for freedom. The War between the states
was marching into newly published history books and into the shielded
conversations of men who did return from Andersonville, Fredericks-
burg, or from the dense cool fog of a Shenandoah Valley.

The color of the sky mirrored the red and yellow leaves still holding position on branches beyond a first frost. Dusk fell, two men sat by
the barn in the fading light drinking hard cider. Spirits rose during this
nightly occurrence at the Connecticut Horse farm where two young
men had labored this past summer into a pleasant memory.

Those who had survived the war, who wanted more than to struggle
with breech block and percussion caps and to keep power dry and car-
tridges from dropping through frozen fingers. The burdened soldier's
wanted an exit from hell - wanted a life with some joy.

A direction west would fit the bill, throw in a long ride on a good horse, adventure, cider, gold, maybe women (thought ladies had yet to be introduced to these men who missed any mixing for most of their youth) war was the bunk mate, shyness set easy with them

"Bet spurs I could reach the Mississippi by snow fall if I was to leave tonight," said J.T. to his friend R. Garth who stood an inch or two taller and was some ten pounds heavier. J.T. tried to act the part of leader, but Garth was a pragmatist, and took time to structure perspective. J.T. could have a plan set but Garth would simply, quietly, and diplomatically point out the loop holes and bring J.T. around. This unusual democratic bond, the two men shared, contributed to the longevity of the friendship.

Garth spoke, his lips just below the wide mouth piece of his cider jug. "Why the hell you planin to ride at night? You can't take but a gallon or two, be gone by morning and where are ya? Just over that hill with damn little in the jug and skitters a buzz-in round your head."

He leaned far forward without full knowledge of the angle his body was taking, until he lost his balance. Then, like the head of a sleeping train rider just before true sleep arrives, he brought his head straightaway and continued his dissertation.

The summer was filled with wooden cider barrels loosing their contents to these thirsty men. This avocation had taken a toll on the ex-soldiers. Too much comfort: beds too dry, food too soft, the morning coffee feeble. It was time to fill their dreams with motion, a motion that would take them west, west to big water.

Their friend, a black man name of Target, had headed south to see his family one last time before again meeting up with J.T. and Garth. He would be the catalyst for this trio, this meeting up would be paramount to the success of this journey

"Can't set off till I strike my deal for that horse," said Garth. Garth had his eye on one of Mr. Camp's best. Mr. Camp, the owner of the farm where they worked, wasn't about to let go of any horse without some fancy trading.

Horse trading was a delicate art for Mr. Camp, practiced with sufficient finesse. So, with his limited funds, Garth would have to amend Mr. Camp's trading constitution to acquire any one of his best horses. A good part of Garth's free time was spent that spring and summer putting in place all the pieces for the ultimate horse trade.

J.T. already had Mr. Five Dollar. He had purchased the big gray from the army a few days before discharge; the gray and he had been together for two years and he couldn't imagine himself without the horse. The army could have given him the horse at discharge but a double-dealer named Upjohn, the Company Saddle Sergeant, convinced the young soldier that five silver dollars would be due before true ownership was his. Upjohn produced an official looking parchment to prove his point. J.T. paid! Upjohn was gone the next day, discharged, only hours after the deal. The incident became a small parcel of army humor for the men who dared to smile behind J.T.'s back. None were so brave as to tease him openly. However the deception gave J.T.'s fine horse his unforgettable name of Mr. Five Dollar.

Sleep came with ease after so much cider as it did almost every night to so many men who were still accountably exhausted from the terrible war that they, and not the others, had lived through. Minutes into their sleep, the arms and legs of these men would twitch, for the war still raged within their body and minds. The virus of so many deaths rushed through the red arteries that came and went directly from heart to brain.

Mr. Camp often joined the men in the early evening parleys. The three men shared a true love of horses and each told his favorite tale of how a horse saved a life or another horse that rode through a fierce winter storm to bring the snow-blind rider back to the barn. The war was mentioned but only in passing, in a fortuitous context. He enjoyed their company and hired them for their ability to handle horses. He too, was a story teller and a legendary cider drinker making the conversations entertaining. A few weeks before the trip west the plan came to Garth to get Mr. Camp tippled, soften his brain to degree that he could slide a good deal past him for his own choice for one of Mr. Camp's best horses.

In the middle of the first week in September Garth set out the dented, trail- worn tin cups, together with some sturdy cider that had been cooled in the spring water of the milk house. Mr. Camp, ever the talker, began the evening's conversation by telling Garth how much he admired the rifle that he had been shown him the first week of his employment. Garth, ever the chess player felt that Mr. Camp, unknowing as he was of the game ahead, led off with a fragile move. Garth felt his own checkmate was but ten moves ahead. He reached forward to fill Mr. Camps cup yet again. Many pints and many hours into the night there two cups rang out in the still night air as they clicked tin against tin sealing the bargain. Garth sure of his conquest, that he was the owner of the best horse this side of Denver. The horse, a majestic gray with a heart shaped shoe on his front right hoof, at last belonged to Garth. The headache that Garth suffered was as monumental as the gray. Mr. Camp, none the worse for drink and pleased that he had a captured audience until dawn, felt he had the best part of the deal. Camp bargained for twenty dollars and a Sharps rifle, found by Garth during a march near Gettysburg.

The Sharps had belonged to a rebel from Chattanooga found dead a few yards off a beaten muddy road, the name of the young trooper carved in its walnut stock, clear and straight, together with the word "Mom" and the date June 9,1864. Garth was gratified to rid himself of this malignant object, a poignant reminder of a war that he no longer wanted to remember.

J.T. and Garth left the Camp Horse Farm the third week in September to begin the ride west. Two men in threadbare but well mended trousers, with deer skin shirts over bleached white skin. They wore large campaign hats that framed their ruddy faces as in a picture by Brady. The horses they rode were the envy of those they passed. J.T. and Garth resembled fighting men even without an official uniform. They sat the mounts like men who were wed to saddles.

It would be a long journey from Connecticut west to the big water. The two had traveled parts of north west the year before. They had returned east, by rail, after taking part in the army's effort to crush Crazy Horse near the Yellowstone River. Most of that return trip was made on a flat car belonging to Kansas Pacific, the small space shared with rough lumber headed to Philadelphia.

They were first-rate civilians now as they moved west again. Making their way without the help of the US army and the cleverness of Target. Target had been J.T. and Garth's master sergeant during the fighting in the north west. The trio had pledged to meet again during the fall of 1869. Target had then continued on going south from Philadelphia to his home, a small farm near Lexington, Virginia. J.T. and Garth rode north to a large horse farm in New Milford, Connecticut near where they ladled away their youth.

The winter meeting place of the three was as vague as the times. Simply put, they agreed to meet on the trail west sometime in November. No formality about it, simply a trail, a city, a month, the remaining circumstances would fall into place without blueprint or discussion.

3

The Ride West

During the ride west it was no coincident that they met many soldiers from their old units. Both had over six years in the service of the North and few men that met J.T. and Garth would ever forget them. In the fighting at Yellow River, the addition of Sergeant Target to this team created a unit that made news, saved men lives, and drove respect into the hearts of the Indian warrior. Few soldiers hadn't heard of this trio.

"Damn if I don't miss that black beauty," said J.T., as he lifted saddle from ground to horse in a long easy sweep. The two were somewhere in the Ohio Valley. They had made excellent time, averaging some forty miles a day since leaving Camp's farm. Little time was spent in any town, except to gather supplies or a jug of whiskey and always to ask a few questions about the state of the nation. The good weather held, little rain, therefore no mud. The night sky was clear and filled with stars. The stars and moon were bright enough to light the trail as they sometimes rode into the evenings.

"I told you before, we'll meet up with that one-armed hunter soon. Sure as, hell won't have an outhouse. He'll find us before we find him," said Garth. They rode over new flat farm land, at times putting the horses to full gallop. They passed through tiny towns where small boys would try to run along beside the horses, their faces filled with excitement. These two men were not the farm hands they were accustomed to, but appeared to them as fighters, true soldiers on magnificent horses, riding through town on some sort of mission. Before the hoof beats faded into the distance, the latecomers would run out from taverns and barber shops and lazy attorney offices and ask the smiling boys " Who was that? Why are they in such a dang hurry?" The boys swore that the one riding the gray yelled, " Just going west." Some also noticed the clear print of a heart shape left behind on the trail. Which of the two horses left such a romantic signature in the dust? No one had the answer.

Those that rode on the trails heading west were looking for something that men throughout history search for after the shock of battle. J.T. and Garth rode to find a new life, for they had witnessed so much. This search wasn't evident to the heroes. It was a mobilization in their hearts that propelled both men. Those they met and talked with, the men they camped with, the men they once fought side by side with, came in and out of their lives during the long ride. Motion somehow pushed time ahead to the next hill where they hoped an answer would be waiting.

When riding they spoke little to each other. At night, once the cheap whiskey had taken effect, the two men opened up, talking until one or the other fell asleep. Their sleep was fitful, for their senses were ever keen to the sounds of the night; like mountain cats they were ready to spring to action at the slightest motion or unusual noise.

Some two days ride from east of St. Louis, J.T. had ridden alone into a small river town to purchase coffee, sugar, and beans. Garth, not of a mind to make small talk with any store clerk, lingered at camp. J.T. returned early, too early to have stopped at any tavern. Garth couldn't hide his curiosity behind the giant mustache that camouflaged his upper lip. "What in tarnation you doin' back in camp before sundown, you must have caught a vapor or you' bein' chased by a ugly woman with a fast horse." He spoke with his usual charm, a charm used to extreme when he wanted to find out a thing or two from J.T. who could be closed mouth when he had a mind to.

"I told you! You whippersnapper, you excuse for rattlesnake meat." J.T. was riled up and yelling to be sure his message wasn't interrupted. "Target is-a goin' ta find us! The store clerk said that a black man with a lame arm riding a black horse to match came through town a day or three ago, Said he was looking for two men riding' west. He said we was so ugly that we couldn't be missed."

"The clerk said he knew I was one of them the black man was looking for the minute I walked in. Now how do you figure that, Garth? He up an knew I was the fella Target was a scouring for."

"My bet is he's a whole lot smarter than you might expect," said Garth much further ahead with an understanding of the store keeper's humor. "What I'd like to figure is where Target could be headin' so's we could be there before him? Just days and the old Mississippi will be comin' up in our sights. Lets take time and look around St. Louis, bet ya my leather boots Target will show up big as life riding that black horse of his. Sure as hell if he's around, people will take notice."

Garth didn't sleep a sound sleep that night, his mind simmered like a full tea kettle left on a back burner, its contents rolling repeatedly, never fully reaching the boil.

His mind wandered the trails taken this recent past. The last three years fighting Indians had filled his head and heart with a respect for what could be called cleverness in war, of fighting using the inventive mind against an adversary.

This was a talent he saw lacking during the Civil War when Garth took part with other men simply marching one after the other, in long straight lines, toward their deaths. Such a bizarre dance to move to on your trip to heaven or hell. Music with heavy base played by cannon, and the high notes of singing men as they shrieked in fear.

His meeting with Target after Lee surrendered to Grant at Appomattox began a creative fighting education. Target was a skillful Sergeant Major who took to Garth and his buddy J.T. Impressed with their bravery, he saw to it that they joined with him and his troopers in the new assignment to go west and fight in the Indian Wars.

After Appomattox, the three men, Garth, J.T., and Target shared many adventures, most of them dangerous yet the only injury among the three occurred when an arrow was left too long in Target's arm, causing nerve damage that left his right appendage limp but his grip intact. Despite this so called handicap, Target was respected by all opponents. He could out- think the attack, overcome any advantage the enemy might have, and strike a winning blow before the adversary was the wiser. His company commander, during one of many decoration ceremonies, said of Target, "This man is the finest fighting man in the Army, this soldier can out- shoot, out- ride any trooper I command and out surmise any Indian in the field of battle."

Garth was up and ready to saddle his horse before J.T. sat straight to rub sleep from his eyes. "Where you going' in such a hell fire hurry," said J.T., it's no more than just past midnight by my reckoning?"

Garth smiled at his old friend and said, "Let's get haying. I got a feeling we might meet up with that sergeant of yours this day and I'm itch'n to get started." J.T. finished the overnight coffee still in the tin pot close to the embers, stood up and relieved himself, and was saddled up before Garth got back from the river with three Confederate cedar-wood drum canteens filled with fresh spring water. By now both were eager to get moving.

The ride into St. Louis yielded news that a black man was looking for two ex soldiers. but Target couldn't be found.

Their friend had evaporated into the fabric of this bustling river city, possibly just around the next corner, but fate wasn't ready to create any meeting just yet. Two days later they rode from the whirling city in disappointment, still optimistic of matching up with the sergeant.

The principal reason that Target couldn't be found in St. Louis was that he had fallen to his appetite for card playing. He was only yards from his old friends both day and night, dealing the rectangle shaped paper in a second- story room at the Blaze Hotel.

He was a sitting twelve feet above the street behind a window that offered a view that J.T. and Garth moved in and out of at least twice during their search. Target played non-stop with the window to his back, his choice of positioning. The back light put him into silhouette making it difficult to register his poker face while playing during the daylight hours, giving him the advantage, he thought. The game was very private and known to few.

He left the Hotel with less money than when he arrived, the back lit seating to create a silhouette hadn't worked. Each hand, each card spoke with mute titles. He felt his losses were insignificant for the money wasn't truly earned, thus his forfeit was of little consequence. The marathon game had helped pass time. His mind employed far from the thoughts of the family that he would never see again.

His effort to find his troopers renewed, Target began to question stableman within walking distance of the hotel. He found one trooper who had seen the two men described, with a slight gesture the man pointed west.

4

Target and the Old Barn

Target had come by this small fortune during his search to find his family in Virginia. After he had left J.T. and Garth in Philadelphia, he rode south directly to the farm where he had grown up. Arriving at the farm he saw that everything, vegetation, buildings, the very ground was still in ruins years after the war had ended. The soldiers from the North had destroyed the area thoroughly in there madness and revenge. Even the trees appeared to speak as though the fire of war left little to live for. A few branches showed the beginning buds of leafs to come. Around the farm they made the only visual efforts of renewed life.

Empty was the mood as Target rode toward the barn, the one building, the one shape, left as he remembered it. The large double doors of the building slid to one side, allowed him entree into a past dimension. Once within, the only occupant seemed to be the mule, Henry.

The mule was an old ally; they both had labored hard for the master. Target accompanied by his horse patted Henry on his skinny rump. Henry made a slow rumble that spoke of recognition.

This barn had been Target's favorite habitat, a haven from the outside. Outside, white men of background and so called "breeding" treated men of dark skin in an unjust manner. His life as a slave was to keep his eyes and head down, to be thought of as an item, less than worthy of intelligence. But he had overcome, he had learned to read under the barn's shelter, made love in it's hay, heard the summer rain beat a thunderous sound on the tin roofing as he read from the classic books hidden in the tack room. Novels, history, poetry all kept there for him by the slave owner who was a man of humanity and vision. The man who taught him to read. A endeavor that was in fact against the law in this southern territory. From the shadows near the tack room stepped the old master with his rifle pointed at Target's head. "What you want boy?" said the frail and broken man dressed in a bedraggled formal suit that once long ago spoke of his exalted position on this Virginia farm. A wore a set of clothes unchanged for years hung from his fragile frame.

"Yes sir," said Target speaking with less than his usually commanding voice. That basic word "sir" used so many times between the two during the years before the war, struck a memory cord in the old man's heart. The rifle dropped ending its leaden ark. The mussel now pointed towards the dirt floor.

"Young Target," said the old man in a familiar voice that Target could never forget. "Could that be you all dressed up like a Union man, blue-black as the feathers of a corn crow?"

"Yes sir it's me. Come to find my family," said Target fixed in his drawl of the past as he spoke to the icon of what his life had been before the Union Army.

The old man began to recount stories of what had happened over the years of war, a beaten man telling Target how the slaves had been let go, how the Union soldiers had plundered the farm, burnt the home, fields, trees and most of the buildings then rode off with the last of the crops in their saddle bags. He had been too weak to fight back, he told of the death of his wife, more of a broken heart than a common sickness. The telling caused the old man to weep, an act that Target had never witnessed in the twenty years living at the plantation. Target could see the war had completely broken his spirit, a spirit that once carried so much authority.

He told of Targets family set free to move on toward destinations with no name or direction. They were now lost somewhere within the vast space of America. What would be there fate? The answer to this question Target would never fine as long as he lived.

Target went to work the next morning with seeds he and the old man found within the barn, his idea was to plant a crop to sustain his friend through the winter. Target also ventured into the surrounding area and found supplies that would feed he and his mentor. He found that a black man was treated with some measure of respect for he had money to spend. But during a blistering hot day the old man took to his bed, never to fully recover from the stroke he suffered while hoeing weeds in the garden he and Target planted. His attempt at re-growth for the farm and the old man came to a premature end.

This fine old gentleman that had been so important to Target, was to die in the tack room where he was a dedicated teacher bringing life to a brain that starved to be filled. His death bed, within the class room, the room where he had spent so many hours teaching reading and writing. He died next to a child's bridle and a tiny saddle that was never ridden hanging on a wood rack just above his head. No precedent to educate his slave, no window to let light in, his reward was to spend his last days with Target, a grown man who displayed, kindness, compassion and empathy. Target told of his success in the army as the old man lie hardly speaking, Target relayed to him how all this was possible because of his teaching and kindness.

Just before his last brittle breath he whispered to Target of a canvas bag of gold coins buried deep under the dirt floor just under the mule, the gold that put Target into the card game that temporarily prevented the St. Louis reunion of the ex-fighting men.

Rain began to fall as he dug a grave for his old friend under the protective roof of the barn. The earth was dry and soft and Target dug deep into the reddish clay soil to best place the old man out of harms way. What better location for his teacher than the class room of his ex slave. After, with his shirt drenched with sweat, his hat in his hand, he walked out into the cooling rain and lifted his face toward the gray sky, allowing the rain to meet and mix with his salt tears.

He packed his things that night taking with him what he had brought and adding to his saddle bag a single book from the hidden shelf in the tack room, Moby Dick, a first edition that the old man had purchased at Harper and Brothers in New York some ten years before the war. During the span of his education, the book was read to him by the old man. Then Target would read aloud throwing his voice to the top of the rafters, as though he were an actor and the barn his theater.

Target stood over the old mans grave that had next to it a small wooden cross with the word "Teacher" carved into it's surface. Target read a passage from the pages of Moby Dick for within was the story of the eternal conflict of man and his fate.

5

Full Moon

J.T. and Garth rode a distance to the north or south of the trail when possible. They were aware of the dangers, mad men, thief's, killers, men from the south who were still fighting all this and more may well await the traveler. Many years in the cavalry can mold a man's awareness, especially when trained by a man like Target. Finding a suitable camp site was always the challenge, looking for water, grass for the horses and safety, all things to reckoned with.

On the fifth night out of St. Louis, camping south off the trail, J.T. and Garth were resting their heads upon sweet smelling saddle blankets, their bed rolls propped against the hulking saddles, rifle at the ready, all making for a comfortable setting. The full moon seemed just above their heads as a lone rider broke the spell, riding into camp as though expected. There was no mistaking the shape or sound of Target. With the nuance of old soldiers, their heads hardly rose from their resting place.

"Howdy, troopers," called the midnight shape. "I smelled coffee and whiskey a mile back. I do believe you cavalry men could use some guidance through this wilderness. With that heart shaped shoe printed all about the trail you were as easy to follow as a steer with diarrhea."

Thus began story-telling that lasted until light, the funniest of which was Target's meeting up with Upjohn, the soldier that sold J.T. Mr. Five Dollar. Target found him by accident working in a small general store in St. Louis. As the story unfolded, it was apparent that old Upjohn had pulled his last trick. From the day after his marriage his new wife placed him well under her thumb; she, not her father, ran the store, and she ran it like a mad company commander. Upjon jumped from task to chore under the high-pitched orders of the shrew wife. Dressed in a peach colored apron worn high on his chest and tied with a small bow just under his breast bone. When they heard this both J.T. and Garth roared with laughter, falling from their perch near the fire. Target would add to the tale as each laughing fit quieted. This continued until both men begged Target to stop, which he did, but only after he had run out of material.

MOON
The moon so often applied as a metaphor
in a poem that murmurs of Love and Desire.
The moon what ever it's nightly shape,
crescent or full, simply persuades the eye
toward the sky.
Passing the stars as though their spark
were too minor to attract notice.
Yet the stars are to wish on,
the moon but a night light for Lovers to
record each other.
I for one will say the moon is the moon,
it is the father of the sky providing
balance to the vastness.
There be no comparison to the moon, its
light is but a reflection of the sun after
all the sun far to hot to persuade Love.
The moon is cool and tantalizing.
The moon is resigned to do what it is best at.
To speak to those in Love.
Speaking of secrets, perfect secrets
that solicit no metaphors.

6

Camp War

The three men left the camp at noon that morning all in fine health, the horses were well rested, the weather perfect, they were together again as a traveling unit heading west. They were so much a part of this United States history, involved in an adventure across what was, in 1869, the unsettled territories, much of it wilderness. The three, moving hour by hour, day to day, planning little yet functioning tirelessly to survive.

The trail sparkled in the early low cast sun light as it reflected off the fool's gold that lie embedded on top of the soil in front of the three riders. The dust of the trail impersonated a beckoning light that directed the three toward a destiny. The air was still cool enough to be comfortable though December heading into Christmas. The men rode, music ringing from their spurs as they advanced.

Though the war between the states was over, tension and distrust were present in the minds of many. The picture of three men in spirited, uniform type dress, one a Negro and a gentleman, possibly even educated, was more than some could absorb. The animosity toward this small company would at times foster a conversation that would lead to questions, then threats, then a challenge. Target, ever the man with a full house could deal to the enemies mind the winning hand. His engaging personality and decorum seemed to be an ingredient that avoided combat. Men, no matter the prejudice, no matter the mind set, can be thwarted by the charm of a well- assigned salesman. Time is what a man like Target needed to win over the prejudices of men that hated other men only because of a difference in skin tone.

It was just such an episode that developed a few nights after the reunion of the three. The camp sight had been chosen by Target during his scouting ahead, scouting that he felt was necessary and liked to do during any movement of his "troopers" as he called Garth and J.T. His selection was a perfect one under a giant sycamore tree near a stream. And as would happen, aggressive, bigoted people wanted to lay similar claim to -the only shade tree near the river. The unfamiliar men rode in just as Target was setting up camp for the soon to arrive troopers.

"Hey boy, what you doing here in our spot? Ya don't want to start no trouble, do ya? Best you move along," said a thin-lipped, light-haired youth dressed in a gray coat that fit the man he appropriated it from far better than he.

"Trouble is a problem that a stupid man brings upon himself when meanness overcomes propitious common sense," said Target standing with both feet firmly planted with arm and hand at the ready.

"What we got here is a smart ass run away slave," said a fat man next to the thin lipped youth. He was sitting on a horse too small and too fatigued for the overweight rider.

"Gentleman, the only running we are to concern ourselves with today is just how fast you both will sprint as you take your leave from my camp," said Target as he moved a slow careful step toward the two.

"This black fool is about to die," said Thin Lip, the upper of which quivered ever so slightly. He then added in a false lower tone, "Which one of us is to have the honor of the deed."

As the words spilled from his toothless mouth one more step was taken by Target. And, in a whisper, Target's gun was pointed directly at the gray cap on top of Thin Lips head. "I'll ask you to remove your hat when you speak to me in that tone," said Target as the gray cap went spinning into the air, dispatched there by perfect aim from his Army Issue Remington 44.

The sound of the shot was heard by J.T. and Garth. Also within hearing was still another man one-quarter mile to the north. J.T. Garth and the stranger arrived at the camp site within a minute of each other coming from opposite directions. A meeting arranged by fate that would change the lives of three men who had fought with the South and couldn't stop their battle. The battle within their hearts lingered on and so they would continue to fight on this day, long after the struggle should have ended.

The leader of the two men, an educated West Pointer, rode into the camp like the captain he was and at once stopped the skirmish by commanding thin lips to retrieve his cap and ride forth fifty yards, and wait his further orders, Without question the ragged soldier and his fat friend did so.

Looking at Target with some respect, the captain asked ever so politely as to the reasons for such aggression. The captain was an eloquent man who prided himself on his ability with the King's English. Little could he suspect that he had collided with a match in the form of an ex slave.

"I dare say my good man there seems to be some sort of difference of opinion, which may merit proper arbitration. Would you be kind enough to explain?" asked the captain.

Target relieved to see his troopers riding in, looking as confident as six soldiers north or south, turned his full attention to the Captain.

"Simply put," said Target. "I have claim to this area for the evening and plan to stay without asking for arbitration, negotiation or, for that matter representation. Your man was of the opinion that I would relinquish the space, but to his chagrin I held all the high cards. And as you may be aware, possession is ninety points of the law." By this time, J.T. and Garth were along side Target, their Winchester.44 carbines cradled in their arms. "Now I ask you good Captain to move along and find your own camp site as you and your band aren't welcome here."

The captain, put off guard by Target's speech, did what West Point taught him and that was to retreat in the face of what appeared to be, unknown depth of an opposing force. He remained ever the gentleman, ask that his men be excused and rode off as though the events were over.

"That was all too easy; the captain will be back!" said Garth.

"Your right Garth these men will return for revenge, said Target. But the captain is wise, and may allow them to vent their hate without joining in the fun. He'll judge the attack, his way of testing our strength, and it's my guess he won't be along."

The fire built that night was brighter than normal, three shapes could be seen under the blankets within its rim of light. Two dead bodies lay as dark shadows beyond.

Target and J.T. had simply climbed into the Sycamore far above the fire, Garth had crossed the river placing himself so as to have a full view of the camp, laying so low that his form couldn't be detected. Just as predicted Thin Lips and the fat friend, minus the captain, sneaked into the outer edge of light, guns drawn. Thin Lips first shot struck the suspected sleeping shape. Garth's two quick shots from his Winchester dropped Thin Lips, who was dead before hitting the ground. Target and J.T. finished the fat man as he spun around looking for where the carbine shots had come from. Neither thought to look up into the tree before or during the attack. Yet in death, their eyes remained open, staring straight up through the branches into the endless night sky.

The captain, hearing one pistol shot and three carbine, and not hearing a pre-arranged signal, was on his way west before the smoke cleared. Captain Mac, as he was named, in his heart of dark hearts had just as surely sent the two to their death. He had used this opportunity to test Target and relieve himself of uneducated men that he hated, did not trust, and feared.

Mac had a spotted war record. His rank had varied from first lieutenant out of the Point through colonel mid-way through the war, then back to Captain after running south when he should have been headed north. He had managed to end up out of the line of fire using his persuasive speeches to attain the advantage, until a company commander by the name of Jackson drew him up short. His last years of service were spent over seeing the frightful kitchen at Andersonville.

"Sure will miss talking to that captain," said Target. "I had some things I wanted to say to him."

"Can't say I took to him the way you did, said J.T. "Somewhat missed him at the party last night," added Garth "We needed a forth, I hate an uneven number at these occasions."

7

Christmas Break

The weather relinquished its imitation of October and was beginning to act more like December. The cold slowed, traveling to a pace far too leaden to satisfy the troopers, and talk of holding up for a spell passed in and out of their conversations. J.T. and Garth were willing to settle down after a short very cold fifteen miles were completed on the trail when Target rode up at a gait nearing a full gallop, he had spotted a small farm ahead and looked excited, unusual for him.

"What's the rush? Haven't seen you this roused since the Yellow River spilled its banks back in 67," said Garth to Target as Target tried to quiet his horse who undoubtedly had caught the fever that his master embodied.

I had a feeling the trail had taken a left years ago when it should have gone right. I liked the look of land to the north and rode that way a few miles, and sure enough came across a valley that called out for a farm. "Troopers, luck is on our side this day," said Target.

"I'm not about to start farmin' in the middle of Missouri just before a snow that will cover a big Indian waist high." J.T. chimed in.

"Hold on to your spurs Mr. J.T." said Target, realizing that more explaining had to be done to capture the interest of this first generation - Irishman.

"What I saw at the bottom of that paradise valley will be to your likin. Being as brief as a man can in this cold, I tell you I spotted smoke from a home fire, I smelled home cookin, I saw a barn built by a talented man and ladies things hangin on the line."

"Well in that case I'll answer for my friend here and suggest that we ride," said Garth as he headed in the direction that Target had just ridden in from.

FALL
The obscure leaf
had still to drop as Indian Summer took residents in the night air.
Drifts of yellow and amber
create a carpet of dry silk under bare feet.
Not long this warmth to stall
blessing the Harvest Moon with soft fog.
Tomorrow or the next
the frost will linger and a
very last floating fleet of color will sail to earth without sound
Tree limbs naked silhouettes in bright sunlight
will rest into winters sleep.
Fall is gone the way of summer --
Oh wait this long winter
for a next warm wind.
Wait !

8

Welcome

M att Wood was walking from barn to cabin when he first saw the three riders heading toward his farm. A welcome feeling filled his heart as not many visitors came this way, especially on Christmas Eve. Matt watched as the trio came closer. He liked what he saw, men who looked noble in the way they sat their horses. The arrivals would be good company for him, men to swap stories with when work came to a halt and snow drifted over the rooftops. After all, living with only women to talk to can soften a man.

"My God, it's you, Target," said Matt in a whisper with the riders still fifty yards out. Matt raised his hand to mirror the greeting that Target gave as he rode up. It was only then that Target realized this person with the welcoming smile was Major Wood standing out here in the wilderness.

It was almost five o'clock and the sun was just below the hill to the west of the farm. Frigid wind followed the men into the valley, a reminded that winter was here to linger awhile, as were the troopers. Luck and good tidings were with them on this Christmas Eve.

"Major, it's been awhile, may I introduce you to my two companions?" said Target, only to be interrupted by the Major insisting that all go straight to the barn where formalities of introduction would take a back seat until the horses were inside, unsaddled, and bedded down. This quickly accomplished, the men looked to the Major.

"Now then, my good man" said Major Wood as he tossed hay to Five Dollar. Who are these fine gentlemen who would be clever enough to bring the once sergeant major out here to Hidden Farm?"

"The trooper with the mustache is Garth," said Target, and the fellow who looks like a friend to all mankind is none other than J.T. Murphy. Both men hail from Connecticut ----"

"Hold up right there, my friend," said the Major again I'll get to know these men in good time. And I can tell from your enthusiasm that I could trust them with my life. Speaking of living, a meal is almost ready and two of the most beautiful woman in Missouri are in the kitchen. I'm sure they both saw you ride up and are fussing around that stove waiting for our entrance. I built a bunk area over behind that wood on the south side, room enough for the three of you with its own iron stove water well and pump just like back east. I'll let you get gussied up and meet in the kitchen in a half hour. Welcome, men. You are a pleasing sight to this ex- soldier."

The barn felt warm, though it was cold enough that the heated breath of the animals filled the air with white cloud shapes, adding a haze to the ambience. The space was awesome, with unique architecture causing walls and animal stalls to fit into expanses that ran this way and that within the area. The barn reminded Target of Virginia, he at once felt safe and at home here. Finished wood was stacked against the south wall, short and long pieces waiting to find their position within the amplitude.

The sweet sound of a Christmas carol coming from a fiddle carried out over the air as the three scrubbed faced men approached the candle lit cabin. A heavy snow fall had began soon after sunset, making there boot prints appear as deep shadows behind them. The heavy foot steps of the three on the cabin porch quieted the music and singing in mid carol, just after the phrase Oh Holy Night.

A glance in the window revealed the major in an enormous rocking chair next to a roaring fire. Coming toward the front door with a skip was a beautiful woman with skin the color of a roasted almond and a smile that could melt silver and gold.

"Merry Christmas," said Brie, to the three men standing in the door unable to move, thunderstruck by the her gentle smile.

"Hell men!" called Major Wood That little gal in the door lacks the desire or strength to keep you all out. Brie, these men represent the

26

army of this Union, men who were instrumental in freeing the slaves. May I present to you and to my wife, Kate, Target, Garth and J.T.. Retreat from your stove and greet these men, Kate."

Kate had been married to the Major for twelve years. He had distinguished himself as a brave and competent officer during the war. He met Target during the battle of Vicksburg, where they spent many hours exchanging points of view while waiting out the siege.

After the war, the major and Kate decided to go west to farm, taking with them their children, two boys and a girl and Brie, Kate's helper and companion.

That first year, three springs ago, five veterans volunteered to go along on the trip, helping the major and his family get a strong start. One by one, all had left to continue their individual journey into the wilderness, but not before the great barn and the four-room cabin were built, as well as twelve acres of land cleared and tilled ready for planting.

Kate came forward, her face a delightful reference to motherhood and charm, she greeted each trooper as though he were a returning hero giving each a hug and kiss. At once Kate had converted the three troopers into the staunchest protectors that any woman could ever want. The three fell in love with Kate and Brie as well as the children, a busy few minutes for any mans heart to rush to warmth.

The room filled with laughter and Christmas carols, the young Wood's allowed up from going to bed to sit on the laps of soldiers and ask questions about Indians. Basic food, a meat and vegetable, a stew that Garth believed was the best meal he had ever eaten, until the apple pie, baked by Brie reached the table.

Garth had been busy at war and never really had time to even look at a woman long enough for desire to mature. But tonight around this table, in this home where love was a anthem sung in a voice heard by the deafest of ears, Garth couldn't take his eyes from Brie.

He was as sure that he had fallen in love as any man can be when struck by such a mysterious bolt. His life, that night, took on a dimension that he never dreamed existed. Brie had become his very breath during a song about three wise men and a star.

Christmas morning saw the snow still falling and the fire in the bunk room almost out. J.T. crept out of bed to put wood into the nickel-trimmed pot stove. The room was soon warm. A shelf over Target's head held coffee and a pot. Fresh water brought forth from the corner well with only a pump or two on the iron handle filled the pot. In only minutes the stove gave up hot strong coffee to bring them into the reality of the day.

Target was the first to speak, for Garth was only capable of laying in his bunk with a grin too large for his face, his eyes focused somewhere in space. J.T. had put the coffee together so felt he could lie until someone other than himself got to moving. Target spoke in a low sincere tone.

"This Farm is paradise. I've not felt this at home for a very long time." Hearing himself becoming nostalgic, he admitted a smile into his pronouncement, "Not since the last time old Garth smiled have I felt so agreeable." Target had looked over at the prone figure of his friend as he was speaking and felt the remark would lighten things up. Or at least cause him to register some sort of reaction. Garth didn't stir. This caused J.T. and Target to fall out of their bunks with laughter. Only with the two of them rolling around on hard bunk room floor did Garth finally give notice that he could be drawn from his dream like trance.

A knock on their door sent the men bolt upright. As they always slept fully dressed. Target simply called out," come in," No thought was given to the command until the figure of Brie stepped forward into the bunk room space. Garth disappeared under his blanket; Target and J.T. sat on their bunks with mouths open, nothing coming out but a whoosh of air.

"Gentleman," said Brie smiling all the more because of this little-boy reaction from such men of combat. She was in total control." It is my pleasure to invite you all to a Christmas dinner at two o'clock this afternoon." she said as she put down a tray of large breakfast rolls on the foot of Garth's bed where he fawned. Faking sleep or absence. "Tell Garth I'm saving a place at the table next to me, I hope he will accept."

At last Target pulled himself together to go along on Brie's tryst - "I don't think Garth would attend this formal dinner as he may not enjoy himself. Beside I don't think he's feeling well, last nights festivities were too much for him." added Target.

A slight movement of the bedcover began. Then a voice somewhat muffled calling out, "Garth would like to come to Christmas dinner. He would sit where ever he was told to sit. Don't listen to Target." Brie winked at Target and tip-toed out of the room. Garth then began still another speech as J.T. pulled the cover from the suffering soul.

"She knew I was here all along," said Garth, crest fallen that he had remained under the blanket unable to look at her.

"Brie played that scene as it should have been played." She not only has beauty but humor as well." waxed Target. Did you see how she put those biscuits right on Garth's bunk?"

"Time to get spruced up," piped Garth as if to try and stop any more comments from Target. "I've work to do before this dinner, some how a bath should be possible. The ice isn't that thick on the pond! Is It?"

When time for dinner had almost arrived the men were ready. All three had managed the dip in the pond, though in all modesty they left their trousers on, scrubbing trousers and all with a homemade soap that Brie had made using herbs that J.T. said smelled like "a lady." "Better than a Buffalo," added Garth as he sung Christmas carols in a voice an octave or two higher than normal, the cold water augmenting his vocal cords.

The festive table was set, the major at its head, Kate at the foot, the kids in their places. Food lined the center portion of the table interrupted only by two large red candles somewhere near the middle; the flame from them seemed unusually bright. All the faces were incandescent reflecting the feeling of the day, the time, the candles, the company. Garth, the last to sit, found his place next to Brie and felt as happy as he had ever felt in his life. "A very Merry Christmas to all," said the major as he looked out over his family and friends. Peace on earth, good will toward men never meant more than it did at that moment in that small room with a warm fire in the hearth, and a full blanket of snow just outside.

9

Winter at
Hidden Farm

The snow that had begun on Christmas Eve continued for a week and a day. Strong winds that accompanied the storm placed the chaste white at different heights, just behind the barn the snow would be six inches deep, but near the front porch it had an altitude of that in feet. Time was spent by the troopers and the major arranging the interior of the barn. There were enough planks stored within the space to work the winter as carpenters. The major was a architect by nature and his talent led the group in innovative directions. Space, once expansive, became unique areas, stalls in a double open fan shape with a center feeding arena, animals looking at one other rather than at blank walls. The pie shape of each stall allowed the animal to lie down on its side the better to sleep. The major appreciated that a horse slept better on its side, so designed for function. Hay could be dropped from above into this one cylinder area to feed six animals at one time.

At the very top of the massive barn was a small widowed room from which a full panorama view of the farm could be inspected. The warm air of the barn rose to this pinnacle as to make the space all the more cozy. Little did the architectural disposition allow the major to realize what a wonderful meeting nook this would one day make. Was it Brie who unveiled the space to Garth, or Garth who showed Brie his lofty discovery above the solid earth. Whatever the turn, this tiny room with a view allowed the two to journey above the questionable world in the year 1870. The magic space was their meeting place.

Brie would knot two small cakes in a dark blue scarf and ascend to the lookout room, a room no more than four-by-four feet square. Intuitiveness played a part in the unplanned meetings. Garth would be there, or arrive only minutes later than Brie. Their meetings came about as naturally as fire light. They talked, smiled, laughed and kissed as blamelessly as flowers blowing in the wind. The cakes were eaten slowly as though to finish them would signal an end of their rendezvous. Time became so precious, each minute, each second looked upon as hallucinatory moments that would disappear all too soon. Reality is elusive when time is so meaningful.

The major was pleased at progress of the barn building made through the month of January. A great deal of the interior carpentry had been accomplished, a feat that would not have been so without Target and his men helping during the winter. He was not unaware of the meetings of Garth and Brie. Kate and he spoke of the two often for Brie had confided in Kate. All was accepted as natural events. Even J.T. and Target allowed things to proceed without any harassment.

January soon turned to February, then March. The snow that fell at Christmas lie three foot below the newest covering. The horses and cows were let out into a penned area on sunlit days so as to muck the stalls and allow the animals to stretch. The exposure to the cold air cultivated the thick protective coats of the animals. The troopers also took short expeditions once a week to stretch the horses and hunt for the meat required for the table. The cellar of the cabin was filled with vegetables, put there at harvest time and kept somewhat fresh within these cool storage areas.

March shook winter hard and left it behind. The snow withdrew as though the ground and rivers were calling with desperation for its water content. On these first bright cool days, Garth took Brie horseback riding. She rode a spry painted horse that harmonized with her dark eyes and hair. A wide red ribbon held hair against a brown forehead, framing a face that artists spend a lifetime searching for. Her smile warmed the March air like a miniature summer sun. Garth gazed upon her as the sun tried to move into and under her skin to reflect back the heat of its existence. She glowed. Garth took her into his arms and kissed

WEST TO BIG WATER

her, the very heat of her filled him with overwhelming desires. Yet the trail called out for him to continue his powerful compulsion to move on with his quest.

The morning after the ride two men leading three pack mules rode up to the barn to ask directions to a nearby Indian camp. They said they had seen a squaw the day before riding a paint horse and wanted to find her village. These men had no idea that this farm was her home or that the man they were chinning to was her protector, to say the least!

Garth asked, "Was she riding alone"? speaking in a tone that let none of his annoyance appear on the surface.

"I believe she was," said a sad but coarse looking man dressed in gray pants and long overcoat that attempted to protect him through the hard winter.

"She was running that paint fast. We was on foot just about to shoot a turkey when over the hill she was a comin." said the second man who sat his horse as though he would jump from the saddle any second. "I'd have to believe she was a princess of some kind the way she sat that horse," he added.

"Sure enough, said Garth, that gal you saw is in fact the full queen of these parts and I'd advise you both to stay clear of her. More than one soldier of fortune has lost his head, just so much as lookin her way. I happen to know for a fact that one young Yankee lost even more, but that's far too gruesome to go into on this fine morning. I suggest that you both continue west and allow that gal as much room as you would a big black bear when dressed in only long-john's and in your hand havin' a knife with but a three inch blade."

The bunk house door opened and the figure of Target framed itself in the vertical rectangle leaving just enough room to see the tiny face and figure of Brie within the shadow he cast.

The two men sitting their horse's looked at the situation as a poker game. The high cards were north of where they were brooding. The only action was to fold and continue west. That day, that face, that skin, the beauty, the simple story of her riding like the wind, though she was nameless to these riders, would be told a thousand times over the years to come. The very tale would be retold to the troopers as they moved west.

It was time to move on west, the three knew it, and the major understood. He did try to change there minds by asking them to stay a few weeks more to finish details within the barn, but to no avail. Good luck and goodbyes were said around a last dinner, cooked with the greatest of care by Brie and Kate. Brie, ever brave, showed no one her sadness.

SNOWING
The window clear and clean
stands between
fire-glow and flakes of snow.
Trees, and paths to conceal,
with blankets of crystal white against
the dark browns of winter.

Bright sun penetrates-
odd that shaft of light to rake the silver flakes
attaching diamonds to the glaze.

Night succeeds
to cloak the blanket's progress
thus the morning exhibits
the trees bent the paths hidden
and the snow endures, the cold preserves
and man simply - looks on.

10

Return To The Trail

Garth had left Brie behind. On the third night away from the farm the thought of not seeing her was too much for him to handle. He rode back over the trail returning East, away from his two friends, toward his love, his one, his being. Garth had told her he would return, yet something was missing in their parting. At the top of the ridge overlooking the farm just after a spectacular sunrise, Garth sat his horse and looked down to see Brie, just then, crossing the yard from barn to house carrying two full pails of milk. He watched her, her way was set responsibility as usual. Unseen, he felt tears fall from his face. He was not aware he had been crying so involved in the image of her form moving so far out of reach. He hoped for her to take another trip to the barn but none came. Just one more time to see her, he thought. It was wrong this looking, acting like a spy. Garth hated this image of himself, he must go. The horse jumped at Garth's slight movement for Garth had not stirred in the saddle for over an hour.

Brie would make her way, he was sure. It was he not she that trembled at their parting. Brie held Garth and told him that no space or time could, or would ever separate them forever. Then she simply told him to return for her when he could.

"See the tall trees, the wide rivers, the mountains and return with stories," Brie said. I'll be here; after all, I wouldn't leave Kate and the kids. Go, Garth, see the Big Water and return for me."

Garth renewed his west by south west heading. Observing his Brie from the distance put his heart into perspective. The trail, the big water, were his obsessions. He rode for three days and two nights to find his friends camped along a small creek,

"Got extra coffee on for ya," shouted J.T., as he looked up to see a whipped Garth ride into camp. Target was half asleep but rekindled enough to welcome him. Not surprised by Gar's arrival, he bid him to sleep late for they would return to the travels the day after. The horses needed the rest and the campsite was a perfect area to complete such a essential assignment.

The next morning when Garth opened his eyes the sun was hot and straight overhead. He felt that its heat had penetrated into his heart, he had dreamt of Brie and the small room at the top of the barn. She was laughing at his attempt to imitate the sound of the horned owl.

Next to the camp site the horses were belly deep in the stream. All were being brushed by his partners, with old Five Dollar nosing his way forward for additional attention. Garth smiled. He truly felt contentment for the first time in many the day.

"You there with the long johns hitched up to your ears. Ya best get out of that water for ya turn into a catfish to be hooked by a prospector," yelled Garth as he finally awoke enough to join the real world.

Target looked toward the lovesick Garth and thought better of saying anything about fish being hooked, whether it be catfish out of water, or troopers sitting in the noon day sun with wide stupid-looking smiles.

The day advanced nicely as the horses rested and the men harmonized in thought about continuing the trip west. During the late afternoon, Target thought that he detected a different odor in the clear air, but his defenses had dulled during the winter stay at the farm and what should have been warning enough passed him by. Target never thought again about the strange smell until the loud thunderous boom of a buffalo rifle was heard about a mile north of camp.

"Garth don't stop to saddle up. Just ride north and see what the hell is going on! Don't mix in -- J.T. and I will gather things up and meet you just west of camp in an hour. Get going!" ordered Target. For as the sound of gun fire reached his ears, he felt that unusual danger was near.

Garth reached the south side of a ridge three quarters of a mile from camp. He approached the peak, dismounting to leaving his horse to wonder about this unusual turn of events. Garth looked over into a small valley of about twenty acres. Milling around and fenced in by hills on three sides were some hundred head of cattle. The extraordinary thing was that, again as many cattle were dead; their bodies scattered throughout the small landscape like so many mortals after a monumental battle of the Civil War scope. Garth fell back from the sight not only because of visual content but from an odor that made his nose react as though fire had been shot into each nostril.

Death, any death, man or beast, left to putrefy, leaves a stench almost beyond the capacity for any person to withstand. Yet there in the very middle, a man on horseback, a buffalo rifle held in one hand pressed hard against his shoulder. The horse he rode was wrapped top to bottom in burlap allowing the animal to appear every ounce as wicked as its rider.

The mans head was topped by a massive dark-colored wide brimmed hat. Under this hat was a large bearded face with wild eyes and a tooth that overhung his lip. The rifle firing, the cattle dropping and were stepped upon by other cattle held within the panic stampede.

Garth rode the half mile back looking for Target and J.T. The lack of a saddle was no problem for his legs held tighter than usual to his horse, fear being the father of strength.

"Death rides a wild horse not a mile away," said Garth in a tone as quite as though he were speaking near a campfire in the middle of the night. "I've never seen or smelled the like of it, "He added as Target and J.T. watched Garth, whose hands shook and whose face was without color. "I'm not one to scream but I was yelling like hell at God on the way here. There is a mad man outright killing animals over that hill and I want something done about him."

"Kill him?" said J.T.

"As sure's a cactus got needles," said Garth.

"Men, I'm all for justice. I want to dig into this just a little more before relieving this mad man from his poor suffocating horse. One long shot from the Winchester and all is finished, all but the questions. Let's ride over and look around, he no doubt sleeps away from the death. We'll find his camp first," said Target.

Part way to the hideous location, the shooting which had continued after Garth left, seemed to have ended. Reaching the spot where Garth had looked over the ridge they all moved with caution to look over into the valley. The first object they saw was the black hat of the mad man. Unfortunately it wasn't at the bottom of the hill. It was ten feet in front of them and four feet of that space was filled with a rifle barrel pointed at their heads.

"Black Hat," as he would forever be named from that instant on, then suggested the three fall flat with hands held in front of their heads. Target was the first to hit the ground pretending he was overwhelmed by the man. Just behind him fell J.T. and Garth.

"I've wondered when this group would be arriving here in my area," said Black Hat to his wrapped horse who seemed to parade just behind him as he moved to tie each of the prone men.

"I've watched you all as you furloughed down by my river. A bunch of loafers if I ever I seen one. Laggards have a way of getting into trouble, the way I see it," added the mad man as he pulled tight on the rope that held Target.

"You're to release these men at once," shouted Target. "They are men of the Forty Third and are under my orders to help in any way they can to round up as many of your cattle as possible and to then proceed to Fort Maggot North of this location. With your help, of course."

Garth twisted his head to look toward Target as he was sure that he had gone mad with his ranting. Black Hat paused long enough to show Target that he may be onto some sort of mind game that could put things right.

"The animals are my property to do as I want with," Black Hat spoke in a low voice cutting each word out, as though made of hot steel.

"My company commander is fully aware of this and has provided me with a set of orders that states your full ownership of all said animals, and his willingness to pay you handsomely for each and every head," narrated Target as dust floated just beyond his lips.

Black Hat walked around the prone, now silent, group. His horse, in costume, to the rear in lock step with him.

"You boys with the Confederacy?" asked Black Hat still spewing words of cold steel. "Ant doing no business with the Gray, not none. Took my horse here not to long ago, afore the winter set in, but I got her back, had to kill the group though."

J.T. shivered as he imagined how many were in that unfortunate group. Had this Black Hat character shot or hung them? Stay calm, he reassured himself, Target will charm him.

Target stated that they were in no circumstance connected with the Confederacy and that he should untie them at once. At last Garth felt freedom as his hands were set loose with the action of a sharp blade cutting through his rope. He rose to his feet and was at once knocked to the ground as Black Hat shoved him hard with the butt of his rifle.

"I'm still in charge," yelled the demented man as his horse rose on it's hind legs to display it's power. At the same time letting out a sound that was unlike any noise Garth ever heard from a horse. It sounded more like a crazed bear, he thought. Garth stayed put.

Next, Target was set free. J.T. was left looking up at the three men after Black Hat told Target and Garth to stand up. Target felt he had to make a move as soon as possible or this irrational Mountain Man could get the upper hand again without warning.

"Your horse?" said Target, "a beautiful and obedient creature. May I ask you where you were able to acquire this mare?"

Target hoped that a conversation about the horse would divert his attention, allowing Garth to bring about a defensive move. The idea worked! Black Hat at once became a horse trader who wanted nothing more than to talk horse flesh, keeping his secret that a sale wasn't possible. He didn't have to walk over to the horse, the horse came to his side as the two men talked.

Black Hat reached up to touch its ear and in that moment Garth rushed to tackle as Target leapt at the large figure both striking at the same instant they knocked the large figure against the horse. The horse rose as before. Black Hat and the two attackers fell to the ground the horse came down hoofs first as Target and Garth rolled to the left and right. Garth was able to get hold of the rifle as it spun in the air. The right hoof of the cloth-covered horse landed flat on the forehead of Black Hat crushing his skull like a pumpkin. The one creature in all the world the felt any kinship with this poor deranged sole caused his demise while defending him. With Black Hat dead the horse continued to rise and fall without direction.

Seeming to recognize his part in the events that unfolded, the clocked creature sought refuse in the valley below. Returning to the death arena below to continue riderless, to ferret cattle until heat and dehydration felled the animal among the many dead.

With bandanas over their faces the three men viewed the final act of the theater of hell. There was but one steer standing as the men turned to bury Black Hat in the shallowest of graves. Hope the wolves and crows find him first light, said J.T.

TREE
A tree strong and tall in the wood.
I leaned into rough bark and felt it's texture at my back
secure now that I could hold my balance
she pressed into me.
I felt the bright sun
her kiss
ripening our body's.
We caressed, the moment everlasting -
wishing for more.
An exceptional memory.

II

New Camp

Damn it, this spot's too close! I feel and smell of that hell hole, Let's move till dark, follow this river for a point far enough away to put this behind us," pleaded Garth. as he knelt on the river bank his head, face and mustache dripping after his attempt to cleanse his face with mud and river water.

"Sounds a likely idea from where I sit," agreed J.T., as Target turned and rode west without a word. Garth had to move quickly to catch up.

The weather turned warmer as the day ended. The clouds on the horizon reflected the setting sun fostering a pattern resembling firelight. When at last a promising campsite was spotted all agreed the effort to distance themselves from the graves of so many was worth the ride. J.T. set about hunting a rabbit or two. Garth built a fire for cooking and baking trail bread, Target rode the circumference of camp to ease his mind.

Morning came and brought with it a renewed effort by the three to continue. The weather was perfect to push the horses hard. They had not been so pushed since last December and took to the challenge with purpose. Deer, wild hog and turkey scattered in the men's path as they rode through the country. There was no stopping to gather food on this day, as distance was the intended objective. The trio was spotted from some miles away by a band of Indians who continued to watch the trail long after they passed. The Indians were sure that whoever was chasing this group would soon follow behind. When no one appeared, the Indians shook their heads and talked of the crazy white man and his attempt to out distance the devil.

The top of a small hill, as it would have been so dubbed back East, presented a perfect camp for the end of a hard ride.

"Sure could see me puttin' a cabin right here, fillin it with kids and a strong wife. I'd spend my evenings sittin' on the front porch lookin out over this here valley waitin' for a bear to go by sos I could ride out and shoot him for my winter coat." said J.T. with a burst of new found bravado. Surprised, His two friends looked at each other and then at J.T. who had taken a lookout stance. His eyes were turned west to the setting sun and the breathtaking view below. In all the time Garth had spent with J.T. he had never heard him mentioned a woman and himself within the same thought. In fact; if the truth were told, he never talked of a woman, let alone children and a homestead.

J.T. Murphy was a man who let others tell tales. He stood with the best but said little. His growing years were Connecticut farm years traveling but ten miles from the bedroom he was born in. In September 1863 his pa drove the team and his only wagon to the nearest train some thirty miles southeast, to Waterbury. From there he rode the rails to New Haven meeting with a group of Connecticut volunteers for the trip south to his first brush with death as a fighting man. He was a good listener, with a quick smile, a brave trooper who could make a trail bread that rivaled any cook's in the Union Army.

J.T. met Garth during his first week as a Union man; they both had like backgrounds drawing them together to tell tales of Connecticut, its winters, the farms, the building of stone walls. No talk of woman, as neither had a lady waiting for his return. This less than romantic fact released them to learn the survival game the better. A man absorbed with thoughts of his gal back home, allowed moments of forgetfulness. In that moment a gray lead minnie ball could penetrate his skull ending the life and the dream forever.

So J.T. watched as another proud sun lowered itself behind the horizon, and he thought his private thoughts. As his fellow travelers scrutinized his silhouette standing strong against the darkening red sky line.

The next few days were uneventful as the trio continued West, J.T. was not to be heard speaking about homes or woman again even though leading phrases were introduced each evening at firelight.

A storm drove into camp cloaked in the self-same wind as the lone rider from San Francisco. His clothing was far more opulent than any the troopers had ever seen. He sat the large spanish mount well; at once, one could detect that the two had been companions for this trip from there to here.

The mount stood stone still as Garth asked the man to dismount and rest awhile. His horse never left the visitor's side and seemed to move step for graceless step with him as he moved forward. The man's trousers were tucked into the top of silver-tipped black seal skin boots. The heal of the right boot was inches longer than normal adding a gate to his movements that caused the viewer to rock his own head in an effort to keep the timing of his motion correct.

"Been riding just ahead of the storm until I crested that hill yonder. Was a counting on you-all would be friendly, an' let me and Violin here hold up till it blows through," said the high heeled stranger.

"That be fine if ya empty that Winchester hanging from the other side of your saddle," said the always tight-lipped J.T.

The stranger lifted the short blue barreled piece from its nesting place tight on the right side of the saddle holding it upright by the walnut stock for J.T. to get hold of.

"I'll not drop this to the ground as this Winchester is one in ten thousand and deserves only favorable handling. I'd suggest one of you fine gentleman handle this with the care deserving a baby girl of less than one month old."

The Winchester as brassy as a young pup. The stock of dark walnut affecting a patina of quality; the blue of the barrel shown brightly in the storm light. A fresh leather string hung from the gold ring nearest the hammer. This was the Winchester of all Winchesters, a piece that any man of war or peace would worship. Its breach hung open as a sign of non-aggression as J.T. reached out to take the offering.

The appropriation of this Winchester created an atmosphere that bonded the men quicker than could be possible under normal conditions. Garth at once wanted to show his traded piece forgetting, for the moment, that he had given it up to Mr. Camp for his mount. Target had a forgettable story about the weapon that had gotten away when the Sioux raided a camp near the Snake River. J.T. held the piece cradled in his lap as the others talked.

The parley came to a halt for the storm was working hard to shift the camp site a mile down range. The wind blew over the green branch tripod set up above the fire, the gallon-sized pot held by its engineering went south with it. Following this first wind came an entourage of dust, debris and branches ripped from surrounding land and trees. The men ran for a gorge just yards south of camp and found the horses already there, even though hobbled, except for Violin who ran side-by-side with the stranger to this safety.

First noting that the storm was winding down were the horses as they lifted their heads to look into the deceasing wind. The men took note and stood to view damage, and listen for a newer unidentified sound.

Scalawags just outside the camp area also waited for the wind to quiet enough to choose the direction toward a planned ambush. They were in fact, the partners of the high heeled stranger, sent into camp earlier with the fascinating Winchester to lull the troopers into complacency. Their plan had been cooked up while the trio traveled west with a small wild animal show that contained a few animated clowns to create the only interest in an otherwise unimaginable show.

Unskilled men with little to do except to wish for money, can easily blurred into a life of chicanery by a wicked man or woman. This their very first assignment would prove not only does crime not pay but that being a clown has its rewards.

This sound made by the hooves of incoming horses was first perceived by Target eliminating any surprise element the clowns thought they might have because of the storm. As the first rider arrived at the camp Target reached up through the still whirling sand grabbing the lead horse by the bridle and pulled horse and its burden down the embankment into the gully. The third villain reined hard left at the sight of his vanishing friend and was out of sight, in the settling dust before any action could take place.

"Grab the horse J.T. I got hold of this fool," said Target as he brushed himself off keeping one boot on the chest of the clown. Off to one side the long heeled one was attempting to mount his horse in rather a frenzied manner. His heal entered the stirrup from the opposite angle. His horse began a light-footed dance, thinking it was time for he and his master to entertain. At the same time, the downed rider next to Target's prisoner had both his hands tied behind his back giggling as only a part-time clown would. This made him appear less menacing as did the dancing horse completing it's awkward pirouettes nearby. The rider sat backward holding on and managing to look as though this all was a planned maneuver.

This scene was all too much for Garth as he wiped the dust and smile from his face. Rather than turn the situation into a showdown he brought things to a halt by slowing the turning horse and bringing the two men together to explain their intentions.

"All a sally?" spoke High Heal in a rather high pitched voice. (a nick name given that night by J.T. to this man with a horse named Violin)

"What the hell is a sally you grasshopper? You hopping into camp to make acquaintances, showing off that damn Winchester, and having your troops follow with evil doing on their minds." Yelled Target loosing much of his cool.

"Sally" is my way of expressing, my pathos for the lightness of which I'd wish yourself and your good partners to receive our witticism," responded the frightened man with the long heeled boot, a smile in his eyes as he spoke. He was attempting to make light of the actions of the hour not only to save his skin, but, in truth to convey his oblique and misdirected activities into the arena of guiltless frolic.

The power of persuasion can be a tidal bore or a trip into a land of charm where the listener returns to reality glad for the trip and wanting to believe all that was said. Here then stood the troopers charmed, believers who held no fear of this man and his forfeited intentions, but rather wanting to discover more. So the three accepted High Heels terms and agreed to meet him the next day at the campgrounds of the circus. To be sure that all would proceed as promised the prized Winchester was kept in Garth's saddle holster.

Garth sat by the fire thinking back over the last week and the uniqueness of its events. High Heel and his jinx were the kind of entertainment that made for a lighthearted visions, welcome interventions that add to the story of ones life.

12

Brie – The Farm – The Fire

The small campfire built by Brie where she and Garth had once picnicked, had burnt itself down to but a few embers, embers that articulated dreams gone by. She remembered with melancholy the day when she, up in the little lookout room, had seen Garth ride up to and halt above the farm. She watched as he and General Grant sat so very still watching the farm. Her heart told her to run from the barn and call out to him. Her pragmatic heart made her go to the main floor to pick up the pail of milk left behind when she retreated to her special space to think of Garth. Lifting the heavy pail of milk she strolled across the yard and into the house. Once inside she walked stoically to her room without a word to anyone, to weep quietly into her pillow. She wanted him so but knew he must make that ride into the farm without her bidding him to do so. Later she stared out the window that contained the view of the hill. However as rapt as her gaze was, she saw no rider on a large gray and had to face the reality that he had ridden on. She understood his momentary return, his desire to see her coupled with his need to keep moving west. Above all she believed that one day they would be as one for a long time.

The farm was enjoying a successful summer; all plantings were thriving. The barn continued to flourish and a string of visitors, old war friends of Major Woods, recycled themselves throughout June and July. One of the many interesting personality was Upjohn the Saddle Sergeant that had sold Old Five dollar to J.T. He had told his wife, at the store, that he was going out for some smokes and had been riding West everyday since. A fellow trooper that he had met not more than fifty miles back had told him of the Hidden Farm and that Major Woods was there. So even though he hadn't served directly with him he felt another Union man could pose upon another in such a situation. Besides he did have some premium tobacco to barter with, to say nothing of some coffee beans that would perk up any early morning conversation dealing with a war story or two. Upjohn was a master at charm, a weaver of tales, to sell, to mystify. He would and could come up to the front rank in these areas.

Upjohn was welcomed to the farm, he helped with work that had to be done, and told wonderful stories on the open porch as the sun set casting long shadows across the barn yard. The children would yell to Upjohn to look at the tallness of their shadows as they waved their arms causing their silhouetted shapes to dance about. He would call back saying they looked like Indians on the war path, which in turn would make them laugh and scream with joy.

From behind the North side of the barn came three shots all with dreadful accuracy, all within the same moments followed by three more only seconds apart. From that first volley and within that juncture six people left this world for the next. The Major his wife, the three children and the old Indian that the Major had welcomed to his family the week before. The Indian was to receive one of the first shots, directly into his heart, the bullet entering through his right side. The Major was next, and then one of the children. The remaining shots killed the others, except Brie who was inside retrieving a fresh pitcher of lemonade and Upjohn, who because of his fortune wasn't on the first shot list. He reacted as the experienced soldier and hit the deck crawling to the door in time to be missed by the last volley except for his ring finger, which was shot clean off. The bullet also took the wide band gold wedding ring that he hadn't bothered to remove. The better to resell it when funds were needed.

The Major with all his combat experience, had overlooked the surprise attack. He had fallen into the complacency caused by the good life here on the farm. All was lost and he had no warning. He or the others never felt the sting of lead for they died before they hit the floor of the porch or the dirt of the yard. No shadow of any length would vibrate from their prone corpses for no one would ever stand to make a long shadow again.

Brie instinctively headed for the root cellar, with Upjohn only seconds behind her. Into the deepest recess they fled, finally hiding behind large wooden bins that were built to hold corn and potatoes. No words were spoken for fear had overtaken all their senses except that of survival. For whatever reason the rebels, who had so massacred the Woods family, did little more searching and remained on the property only long enough to start the fires in and around the barn and home. Then, led by a Captain Mac, rode off like so many manual laborers, to return to their homes somewhere in the South. Back home to Dixie Land feeling justice was done in the case of this Yankee Major.

The magnificent barn burned like it was a torch meant to signal all the hatred of mankind. Within minutes, even before the assassins were out of sight, the barn fell onto itself board by board in turn each and all consumed by flames. It was whole and then it wasn't. The little room at the top, so treasured by Brie and Garth, created a chimney pulling hot air and flame up and out, the better to make it all disappear. All animals were away from the barn because of the warm nights, so lived to see and, like Brie and Upjohn, not fully understand what had happened.

When Upjohn heard the roar of the flames he knew that he and Brie had to get out or they would suffocate. A run for their lives had to be made. So even before the fire took over the slower-burning house, the two had run out the rear door hidden from the retreating men by the structure itself. They fell to their knees in the middle of the garden further hidden by the second growth of sweet corn.

The immature corn caressed Brie's cheek. To her muddied intellect the corn resembled a cool safe place in which to stay but the pull on her wrist by Upjohn awakened her to the horror of the bullet. Upjohn dragged her at a pace faster than what she thought herself capable of. Out of the corn, lurching and stumbling over the hill behind the now incandescent house and barn. The two hunkered down for what seemed hours until they were certain that the Rebels had taken their leave. Only then did Upjohn thrust his head over the crest of the hill to assess the horrific damage done to their lives and loved ones.

Upjohn instinctively thought that the farm should be put as far behind the two of them as quickly as possible. With some effort, his finger still bleeding, he managed to capture three of Major Woods horses, allowing the remaining animals to go free, and before darkness had settled in he and Brie began the ride west. A direction opposite the bloodthirsty renegades.

The vacant opaqueness of night advanced as the fires consumed the wood structures drawing a blackness over itself as the flames dwindled to tiny sparks, then to embers and soon into darkness. The noble buildings were gone forever, time would destroy all trace of this small settlement of Major Woods.

In the years ahead only this odd break in the trail would effect any inquiries. Within a decade new growth would complete this space as though it never existed. Like so much of all wars much has been left behind, much has been forgotten.

Lost civilizations

THE MIND SLEEPS
Lifeless
The mind sleeps
to hide
I fall not feeling
cry not hearing.
I saw you and
there was no life
your voice gone your kiss cool
I strive to loose this sadness
when sleep chances.
Your touch was life .
To see you
was to bring wind - sound - the sky
all that is correct into center.
All this lost —

49

13

Exodus

Now the trip West became the primary thoughts within Brie's heart and body. She must face this adventure for Garth was out there. She had a direction an objective and she had the greatest of longing, a love. Just to see him again to feel his hands and lips, to hear his voice in no more that normal conversation was all she could think of at this moment. To contemplate more would surely drive her out of her wits.

"We are going in the right direction aren't we? "she timidly asked her savior, the still-shaken Upjohn. His fore arm wearing a tight tourniquet created with a blue bandana to avail the bleeding of his lost ring finger. An important keep sake of Brie's used to hold small cakes to carry up to the top of the now lost barn. One day she would have Upjohn return it to the rightful owner.

"Well, if it would make you feel any better we are! From what I have decoded from being around you these past weeks and from what Major Wood told me, Bless his soul," said Upjohn, as he crossed himself though formal religion wasn't part of his chronicle. "You my dear are in a stampede to catch up to that Garth fellow."

Of course Woods had told him nothing of about Garth and Brie, but the conniver sounded full of facts and pushed for information much as he had seen his wife do day in and day out back at the general store.

Soon, more than she wanted to tell had spilled out in a true confession-style that left Uptown with a renewed responsibility to get this girl and her man back together. Hidden within his materialistic personality lie a romantic, a quality he was unable to express in his own relationships.

On the third morning of trying to put the killing and burning behind them, the two rode bare-back into a small town, called Big Spring some twenty-five miles west of the farm. Brie knew of a merchant named Wendel Gates. She had met him on the day he delivered a large wagon of supplies that the major had ordered. She and Upjohn found the general store and encountered Gates sitting tipped back in his wood chair watching the dusty street and their approach.

"Well hello there little one, said Gates." He stood to take a closer look, for the two riders appeared drained and covered in dust, to the point of wearing an unwanted disguise.

"What in the world has brought you here?" asked Gates as the two reigned their horses at the well-worn fence rail of the general store.

"We come with tragic news death, burning, a massacre at Major Woods ranch," babbled Brie as she fell from the horse into the store-keeper's arms.

Following a twelve-hour sleep at the only hotel in town, Brie told Gates what had happened at the hidden ranch, how she and Upjohn had to escape without a proper burial of the family.

Gates dispatched a three man crew to return to the Hidden Ranch and see to it that proper graves were dug and a family head stone placed along the trail as near to the cabin as possible.

In the mean time, Upjohn was at his best in the tavern trading one horse for another until he wound up with two rather good riding horses plus two pack animals and saddles. His trading was augmented with some cash given him by Gates who held the amount as an unused credit in the Major's account. Gates, the wise man that he was, gave Upjohn only enough for him to trade for horses and supplies; the remainder was given to Brie with a word of caution to hold tight to the amount without telling of its existence.

Two full days after riding into town the pair were well rested, well supplied and off to find the trio from the East. The odds for catching up to their friends might be beyond comprehension but innocents can be a blessing in such a situation. As they rode out of town Gates looked on and somehow wished he, too, was going on such an adventure, He vowed to one day meet up with Brie in San Francisco.

Less than a week later Gates was to be face-to-face with Captain Mac who alone rode into town after a separation from the killers he had recruited to take part in the eradication of the people at Hidden Ranch. A revenge slaughter that was meant for the three troopers that had underestimated his hate at the camp some miles east of the farm. A small conversation around a campfire with disassociated men that told of the black trooper and his arrogance at the farm led Mac to the confrontation. Gates, not aware of the true evil of this man who spoke with excellent manners, sold him his desired ammunition, hard tack, flour, and coffee. Gate asked him if he was, in fact, heading west and his answer was simple put. "I'm heading to the fine city of San Francisco."

14

Return to Circus

The entire circus was bedded down in a small well-sheltered canyon north of the main trail. The old camel named Oboe greeted the three with a blast of bad breath. High Heel came skipping to them with his inevitable charm surrounding him like a befog of silk. He seemed so pleased with himself and at once asked after his prized Winchester which lay with a shell in chamber across Garth's saddle.

"Are you up to any barnyard tricks on this fine morning?" Garth asked more in self defense than for any other reason.

"What has been done in the past by this pitiful soul is to be forgiven and forgotten by all and in particular by you three who I have grown to love and respect above all men past and present," pronounced High Heel in as sincere a voice as was possible under these circumstances.

This type of declaration fetched grins to the troopers faces for the word "love" was rarely used by these men. Though they had encounter so much throughout the fighting years, delicate speech wasn't one of their cultivated facets.

High Heel paid little mind to any reaction of the three for he was into himself and therefor only heard his own voice or saw his own shadow.

"Allow me to offer you the grand tour of this celebrated traveling show," piped the original Pied Piper of the West. The glorious invitation caused the three to dismount their horses and joined this showman as he went from freak, to midget, to animal, introducing the men as heroes, horsemen, as soldiers. Near the end of this grandiose display Garth was convinced that the adventure at the camp site was an acqui-escent enterprise that should be overlooked.

Upon completion of lunch consisting of buffalo steaks and hard trail bread dunked into a pail of thick gravy, the group assembled at the edge of the compound to say there good-bye's. Garth had holstered the Winchester, not offering to return it, nor did High Heel asked for its return. So off into the mid-afternoon sun rode the three, a fair trade thought Garth as he removed the pre-loaded cartridge from the breach his Winchester.

The distance traveled over the preceding weeks had been limited by most standards. No mention of this had been made by the three. On the other hand Brie and her traveling companion were making no attempt to drag their feet, moving at a pace that would make a cavalry company green with envy. They would catch up to the traveling circus six days after Garth placed the Winchester into his saddle holster.

15

Brie at the Circus

High Heel first saw Brie as she rode toward the tents, silhouetted against the setting sun. She was as, would be admitted by any man, a beauty that halted heart and blood for a moment as the mind focused. Brie was curious as any young girl would be after seeing her first camel and missed the missteps of High Heel as he approached her. His opening conversation filled her mind with information that was wanting. He confessed that she and her companion were the first visitors that had wandered into there space sense the three men, one a black man had rode off not more than a week before. The circus had not moved on, added High Heel, because of a virus the camels had contracted, their coughs echoing in the background, confirming his account.

Brie turned to Upjohn, who was still impressed by the camels and had listened with only half an ear to what High Heel had said. "Upjohn, please, we must continue now," said Brie. Her face flushed with the thought that Garth was but a few days away.

Before Upjohn could answer, still half brained with the camels in his head. High Heel injected an invitation to stay the night and swap stories. He had already decoded that this duo knew something about the troopers who went west with his Winchester. He began a campaign to keep the two. It included a special meal, and the promise of detailed accounts of the three troopers. The invitation was reluctantly accepted by Brie and welcomed by Upjohn who was ready for a chance to talk of bartering of any description.

Upjohn tried all his techniques in order to trade a horse or two and a gold watch that had been a wedding present from his wife's family to acquire one of the camels, sick or well, fat or thin, but to no avail. A camel in any condition wasn't to be had. High Heel wasn't in a trading mood his motives were of one dimension the whereabouts of the troopers.

As the night wore on, High Heel leaked bits and pieces about the trio. Brie would take in every word without disclosing her all-consuming interest. She wanted to divulge what she knew but dared not for his true motives were unknown to her. His concern dealt with the missing Winchester and its eventual destination. As he spoke, not more that a three day ride away the weapon in question rocked along side the saddle that sat on the horse with the heart shaped shoe.

The next morning Brie convinced Upjohn that they must be on there way or lose all chances of catching up to the troopers. Using her feminine logic she defused all of High Heels energy to slow their progress even having him pitch in some extra food supplies. She reversed his logic that their catching up would help his cause. His last wish, as he called it, was that Brie remind this wondering troika that he had not forgotten his Winchester was in their possession and that he wished for its return.

By nightfall, Upjohn and Brie were miles away from the traveling circus. They were not aware that during the morning of their departure High Heel and his band of cohorts, animals and all, were making the decisions to return West. High Heel had to allow that in the best interest of animal health, this was the better direction. The very backbone of the circus, was the living breathing, roaring, animals. He convinced himself that this appraisal had nothing to do with his legendary Winchester.

As Brie lie in her blanket a week later, she felt that Garth was some where near, thought in fact he and his troop were separated from her because of a parallel trail. Where she and Upjohn had taken the southern route, Target had elected the less traveled trail to the north. So in fact they were close to each other, side by side, but apart, for each thought one was behind and the other in front.

The moving of a tiny circus in the 1870's demanded Herculean efforts, packing up wagons, animals, food, to say nothing of convincing the roustabouts that returning to what was an unsuccessful area, where wages had been suspended, was the sensible direction to follow. Who but High Heel could complete such an effort. And to the surprise of even the most resistant, the show was on the road in two days flat from the morning Brie and Upjohn left. The camel who was in the poorest health seemed to rise to the occasion and trotted down the trail as thought show time was but hours away. The lion, encased in his well-decorated wagon, though old and tired seemed to react as though this movement was in his best interest and therefore put forth a giant roar which caused the coyotes to wake from there early morning slumber to listen, look, and wonder.

SPRING
Spring arrives on the stern of winter
its heat pressing against the walls of March.
That first glorious day- this marvelous new warmth
seems as though its always been, until
the chill night blocks the celebration.
Let us retire to a benevolent zone - Renounce!
Take our warm heavy coat
put it in a closet- forever.
Pack the achromatic color gloves,
the knitted pull over cap smelling of moth balls,
and stale pipe tobacco.
Put them all in with that Zen book you never read.
And drink warm gin as you smile
toward the spicy sunset that remains.

16

Pony Express

The Pony Express, the newest of mail systems was beginning its colorful history. With it came way stations where men and horses were rested and fed. Into this pitiful oasis rode Brie and Upjohn thinking only to stop, rest a bit, and move on. Where one man sees only dust another perceives gold; where Brie felt comfort at this outpost Upjohn felt opportunity knocking. Conversations with the station operator indicated that the system was hiring, needing both riders and station operators. Upjohn wanted to sign up at once, Brie pleaded that he must accompany her to San Francisco as he had promised.

Upjohn signed up and after hours of haggling Brie was convinced to become a messenger for the Government of the United States. Brie would change into the clothes of a dead boy who had been killed by an Indian arrow the week before. The boy had ridden into the mail stop with his pouch of letters safely on the saddle, the arrow still protruding from his back only to die as night fell into total darkness. Another boy lost in the fabric of the of history of the west. Brie, would take his place to continue her journey. Brie left the station to the capable hands of Upjohn, its previous employer heading east to relieve another. She had her direction, a wonderful horse and a pounding heart for she felt that this was the express way to Garth's arms.

Brie would ride for the system, leaving that very morning when the rider coming east rode in. She was to continue riding west, changing horses every twenty miles, her light weight, her youth, her spirit, all combining to the make her efforts, a success. The truth that she was a beautiful woman hidden in the cloths of a dead youth, that the shirt she wore had a patch framed with a large blood stain that wouldn't wash. That her hair was tied in the back, her glowing skin covered with layers of dust made her look the part of the genuine male Pony Express rider with no apparent family background, simply a reckless youth who worked for the government.

Reality stumbled into focus as she crested a small hill and saw, not a mile away, Indians trailed by a large cloud of dust indicating that this party was of significant size. She instinctively knew that if the tribes were out their braves were in front scouting. This no doubt meant one or more was very near, maybe watching her at this very minute. She back tracked a bit and hunkered down in a small draw off the trail. The horse seemed to welcome the rest time as the groups of Indians passed. When the dust settled back on the trail, Brie remounted her horse and was off at a full gallop. Behind her was the first scare, and an hour lost. She had acted with an intuition that surprised even herself.

A very young brave had seen her retrace her steps to hide but elected to avoid any conflict that might bring revenge to the tribes at large. He watched, waited, and moved off like a faint trail wind.

Brie reached the first station and within minutes changed horses, drank from the well, said little and continued on. Few words were spoken for she was still training her voice to sound more like the young man she was impersonating, but dared not test its tone on this first stop. Her next stop was thirty five miles ahead. Her load was only the leather mail pouch, two full canteens of water and some beef jerky. She was assured that water for the horse could be found along the trail.

She rode alongside a wagon train that harbored some people in pursuit of the magic West. She passed a lone family, who had been separated from the train because of bad blood, owing to a horse and chickens and who belonged to who. Though if the truth were known, the wife of this lone family may have spent a few midnight minutes with the husband of another woman and thus was asked to voluntarily leave the train.

Brie thought of little as she rode through full daylight except the distance between she and Garth. In the mean time, Upjohn had begun his tenure as the station operator. His head filled with ways to profit from this position laid in his lap. He felt no regrets as to his abandoning Brie. After all, he reasoned, he had helped to get her this far and she was well on her way west with a paying job to boot. His first thought was to arrange to be the overseer for this post so that he may turn it into a general store to sell goods to all sorts of people heading to the Pacific. He even thought of contacting his wife and her family, having her forward goods, on credit of course, to begin this venture. On second thought he concluded that a reexamination of the plan was in order. There were ways of having goods shipped. However ready cash or credit was needed, he would need time to draft this project.

Brie continued to ride hard toward the next station in what would have been classified as record time had any one been marking the event. Here she was to rest and return back into the direction she had come as the rider from the west arrived with the mail pouch going east. He was to return west the next morning carrying the pouch she had brought along. She convinced the waiting rider to stay on, having him take her post, so she could continue in her rightful direction. She faked her slumber until the post grew still with sleep.

A fresh horse was led from his stall into the night. She rode at a walk until first morning light at which point she and her horse began an all day trot arriving at her next post just before dark. Here she would sleep through the night after surrendering to a fine meal cooked up by Old Mike a friendly retired union sergeant. He wanted to tell his stories to the fresh young ears, but the ears and the youngster wearing them, fell asleep mid tale. He did in fact know of Target and his troop, the three had run into his post less than a week past. They, as Brie, stayed the night, enjoying the tall tales of Old Mike.

Apparently awake the next morning, though somewhat groggy, she led her horse to water. Her mind and body preparing for the ride ahead. She chanced to look at the markings in the soft mud about the watering tank. There her eyes met with the clear heart shaped shoe design of Garth's horse. The print was kept unaffected the last few days because of the inactivity at the station and the stale water that postured in it's cavity. Her breath became uneven for what seemed like minutes. Was this what it meant? - Garth was here recently, she screamed - then at once despaired that the station operator would hear a woman's voice.

She must ask questions- she must fine out anything that Old Mike would know. She settled her horse to the pump with a flip of the reins and ran to the outpost building sprinting smack into Old Mike as he headed toward this voice of a girl.

"Mike," she cried, "was a man named Garth here? -tell me -tell me" forgetting her bluffing ways.

"OK Miss said Mike, first lets put the horse under the shed and go inside for some strong coffee and flapjacks. I can make more sense in the shade, I always say."

The table was set, tin plates next to oversized forks, even a union blue, well worn napkin, was next to Brie's plate. A large pot of coffee called out with its aroma for the two to sit and talk. Old Mike was first to speak as Brie was still shaken from her discovery of the heart shaped hoof print.

"First out of the stall, said Old Mike, "I knowed right off you was a gal the minute you rode in, you're too pert and walk too smooth to be anything but." Brie looked up at Mike, took her head covering off, allowing her hair to fall around her face her eyes warmed the old man, he continued his speech.

"This fella Garth, guess you saw the heart in the mud, I took to that shape kept the horses to one side this week so as not to run it over. I spent a week of Sundays with him and his crew up around Snake River awhile back. The kind of fellas you don't soon forget. They showed up here on their way west, got them to stay over, needed friends like them to talk to, it's a lonesome job this here post. Well getting to the center of the pond all the rest of them farmhands fell asleep as I was telling my tales except Garth, I talked awhile and he started to spin this here tale about the most beautiful gal in the world left behind at a farm some place East of here-I took it that he had far too much bad whiskey and lost his mind. To tell you the honest truth ma'am he was one trooper lost in the desert of love sickness. Kept telling me he was about to return east and put you on his horse and bring you west. Well after an hour of this here romance talk I put him into his bedroll still talking, the next morning he said nothing to me about any of this. Last night you come a riding into post looking ever so like this lady Garth was a rambling about. So I put one and one together without so much as a stick of proof except that he had said you could ride like the wind. Not many can ride so well but you could, and I knew then you were Garth's woman in a boy's outfit."

Old Mike stopped to take a breath.

Brie sat up straight looked at Mike, without a smile and asked in a slow deliberate voice. "Which direction did the trooper go, how many days ahead are they? I am no longer a pony rider, can you pay me any wages earned, can I take the horse I rode in on?"

Old Mike liked the cut of this gal, and proceeded to do everything in his sway to send her on her way to hook up with Garth. Old Mike understood her as though he was lodged somewhere inside her heart and brain He was unable to pay any wages due, but did let her claim a horse as she had left he own at the first station. Most important she was given the important provisions, an directions to keep she and her horse operative on the difficult trail ahead. She rode as though she were free for the first time, her head cleared of all questions, the horrid happenings at the ranch pushed deep into her memory bank, her feeling of being lost within this great expansive land were all behind her. Brie could only think ahead. She felt Garth was so close, just over the next hill, just beyond the pass. She understood that her horse was just so strong and must not be rode like a pony-express animal. The strength of the animal must be conserved, dolled out like so many rations so as not to use them all up before nightfall

17

Garth and
a Foul Rabbit

Garth rode with an uneasy feeling in his belly, the rabbit J.T. had shot the night before was getting some sort of revenge on him. J.T. was up ahead seemingly no worse for wear. Target had long ago moved on ahead to scout. Garth's thoughts so often with Brie felt that much stronger this morning despite his uncomfortable mid-section. The visit with Old Mike a few nights before made this vast country seem smaller. From out of his war years came a familiar face that he had assumed he would never see again. So many faces through the years, faces and voices that deserted, that were discharged, that died. These faces were put out of mind, to recollect brought pain and discourse, a sadness that was foreign to him. His longing for Brie lifted his heart, her image generated energy propelling him through each day. Though apart he had no misgivings that he would be at her side again.

The pain in his gut persisted all day, by night fall after refusing supper other that some trail bread dipped in his over sweetened coffee, he complained to his partners for the first time about how he felt. "I feel like old five dollar kicked me full in my gut after being bit by a yellow jacket," said Garth his face the color of white desert sand. "I don't cotton to being out here in the wilderness sick as a dog." Target took a closer look at his friend noted his ashen look and suggested he try to get a good nights sleep and evaluate his condition at first light.

63

Target was worried but chose not to further alarm Garth. During his up ahead scouting that day he had come across a rather large wagon train. Though he didn't make contact with them as he watched from a distant hill, he was sure that some type of medicine man would be with so large a train. Just before first light whispered to J.T. to hold camp until his return hopefully before high noon. Target rode out to pursue the wagon train to fetch what ever medical help he could fine. He reached the travelers camp before they had begun the morning move. Target located the wagon master who he discovered he had served under in the early years of the war, A well respected colonel from Ohio who had left West Point in his junior year to fight for the North.

After a brief reacquainting Target's problem was addressed. A wagon filled with straw pulled by two strong mares were dispatched by the colonel together with an ex army medic as it's driver. His orders were to pick up the wounded man and return to the wagon train by the next sunset. The wagon train moved at an average eight miles a day over the flat land. This assignment to catch up would be an easy one.

Into camp rode Target and his newly acquired team of horses and wagon together with it's gray bearded driver. Garth was sitting up, his back to a tree looking weak but improved after spending the day emptying his body of almost every once of fluid top and bottom. The medic offered a green tea he had in his bag of tricks. J.T. already boiling water for evening coffee handed him a tin cup of hot water, health for Garth was not far away. The tea was sipped by Garth before the tired horses from the wagon joined Mr. Five Dollar and Garth's majestic gray, General Grant, for a much needed drink and cooling down in the near stream. A stream that ran it's task of rolling on day after day joining the passing of time with it's motion. It's clay shore mirrored recent prints of horses hoofs pressed into it's mud like surface. Notes left by those that had visited it's banks for a cool drink.

18

Another Heart Print

The large tree near the stream where Garth began his recovery from the illness was a welcoming picture, a perfect resting place for Brie as she unknowingly closed the gap between she and Garth. Her horse picked up his pace the better to reach the water for a much needed drink. She thought that this ideal location looked to be a fine place to camp the night even though it was still early in the afternoon. A good rest would be a smart thing, after all she and her mount had been pushing rather hard for sometime. She dismounted and allowed the horse to get to his water, leaving the saddle in place. After a look around Brie went to the edge of the stream to splash her face and fill her hat with water then placing it on her head allowing the water to flood her hair and run down her front and back. The heart shaped hoof prints were there, they were all around her, yet pre-occupied with her cooling off she didn't notice marks in the clay. She walked the horse back to the tree and removed the saddle, throwing the saddle blanket over a near-by tree trunk the better to dry in the sun. The saddle was placed at the base of the tree that Garth had attempted his recovery, it would be used as a pillow when she got to rest. One more trip to the edge of the stream to fetch water for cooking and then to sit and think. There she at last noticed the prints of Garth's horse, so many, so perfect, he must have camped here, she spoke in a whisper so as not to disturb the vision, She looked over at her horse as though to say are you ready to move?

Garth was only a day or two's hard ride ahead mixed in with the giant wagon train still recovering his strength. Brie was aware that he was close judging from the fresh look of the prints. A becalming wave came over Brie, a feeling that all is well, a feeling she thought she has lost minutes after the massacre at Hidden Farm. If Garth was near, a bath in the stream would be a good idea and the resting of her horse and herself was also essential, only a few hours and she would be on her way. She tethered her horse where grass was plentiful and proceeded to shed the boy look and return to that of a woman. After washing herself and what clothes she had she turned to making a light supper of hard tack and rice. She so wanted to get started before dark but lie down for a moment and awoke ten hours later.

She hadn't slept that completely in a long time. She felt renewed, even her horse seemed ready to move though the suns light was but a soft glow behind the horizon line. Little could she know that before the moon could rise into the night sky that she would be standing beside Garth holding him tight to her body, feeling as though they had not been apart for more than a few moments.

The wagon train had bogged down at the edge of a swift running stream the majority of people in the train had voted to wait out the passing of high water believing that it would lower itself several feet in the coming twenty four hours. This wait time would be well served for in the past the attempts at crossing too deep a river caused loss of wagons or live stock. This wait time also would allow Brie to catch up to Garth who had remained bedded down in the wagon of straw. He was sturdier, simply weak from the lack of a full meal.

Garth was sitting at the end of the wagon his stocking feet hanging over the tale gate when he spotted the lone rider silhouetted against the still bright evening sky. The rider moved along the ridge line as though looking over the entire camp to best choose an entrance point. The shape of horse and rider awakened Garth's mind. That is Brie, she who filled his mind most of every day was out there, too far away to call to. He felt weaker than he had, his heart beat was faster than normal. Just then Target rode up in front of Garth and jumped from his horse.

"Get on and go to her." said Target. "I have followed her for the last hour not wanting to be the first one to speak to her, just to make sure she was heading in the right direction."

Garth, with poised difficulty, mounted Targets horse without words or boots or hat and rode straightaway to her side. Brie saw Garth as he worked his way toward her, sliding off her horse she was standing tall as Garth rode up. He looked down at he face which like his was filled with happy tears he slide from the horse's back and into he arms.

They spoke little, except for single words repeated over and over: wonderful, happy, always. Then Garth ask the key question, "how did you find me?" A question that Brie simply answered by saying, "We shall speak of that story later."

Brie ask about his frail condition which Garth explained by saying that the fault lie with a rabbit not getting along with his insides. Shortly Brie became busy nursing Garth back to normal. Rest, mixed with Love and a magic broth she created put Garth on the path back to perfect health within twenty four hours.

In order to keep a distance from the many questions and excitement of the upcoming river crossing, the two set up camp a half mile up stream. Garth slept much of the time growing stronger with the passing of each hour.

Brie began her story of why she had arrived so far from Hidden Farm as Garth became himself again. The ambushing and burning of all that was the Wood's home stead came first, then the killing of the entire wood's family how Upjohn helped to save both there lives by running through the corn field. Upjohn's rounding up of the horses for them to ride to the nearest town to gather the help of Gates the store keeper.

Garth was so stunned with horror that he fell silent as not to disrupt her fast paced telling of her sad adventure. Questions could come later he thought as he took in each word. When she told of putting on the blood stained deer skin shirt of the boy killer by an indian arrow he almost interrupted but was stilled with Brie putting her fingers gently upon his lips. Brie told the entire tale in only minutes, ending with the seeing of the heart shaped print a days ride from where they were camped.

More details would divulge them selves as the days and weeks pasted. All Garth could think of was she was at his side this very moment and what a miracle that would always remain.

As Garth slept Brie took the opportunity to ride back to the wagon train to pick up flower and coffee, as well as some buffalo meat. She spoke to J.T. and Target about riding up to the camp after their evening meal for a visit. They happily accepted and sure enough the entire group came along in Daisy's wagon that Target had arranged to bower before dark settled in. The asking of Daisy's wagon became Target's job as J.T. was still too shy to ask her. All were cheerful sitting around the wonderful camp fire built by Brie the better to see all the smiling faces that would cheer Garth. J.T. had brought along a small jug that was sipped by all except Garth who felt weak enough that he dare not sample that warmth.

Daisy and her son were introduced to Brie with little fuss or details and was accepted at once by Brie as a friend to cling to among all the fabulous three that she felt so close to.

19

J.T. – The Romance

J.T. had found his way into a group of men within the wagon train as the time passed waiting for the river to concede, they used up the clock by resting, talking a little about the war, and most notably card playing. A fellow named Miles Stepp whose sleeve accommodated a hidden card lost his life when it dropped onto the blanket that served as their playing surface. It should have stayed in it's resting place where it would have been used at the appropriate time. It's appearance caused a hot headed loser to shoot Stepp dead, without discussion, where he sat.

The wagon master and a small group of dignitaries chosen by the people to make ruling in such matters, sent the slayer on his way, banished from the train he rode off into the night sky leaving behind nothing but a pack of marked cards. Along the trail west he was recognize hanging from a study branch, naked except for one well worn boot, it was but a month to the day that he had rode from the camp. His cessation were never establish, such was the story of so many during this time in history.

The shooting of Stepp left behind a widow, a two year old son with a permanent smile, as well as a covered wagon three strong horses, and sundry supplies. Mrs. Daisy Stepp was a handsome and capable woman who hadn't made the most prudent choice when she married. Daisy was a young girl from a small farm village out side of Philadelphia. She was no more than twenty two the day she became a widow.

Despite his shyness J.T. wanted to speak with her after her husbands death to convey his genuine sympathy. He had encountered her but a day or two earlier when Stepp brought him over to their wagon in an attempt to trade a worthless Civil war item for J.T.'s brass handled pocket knife. He had invited J.T. to play a hand or two as he thought he would be an easy mark. J.T. returned to the Stepp camp to play cards only on the chance he would see Daisy again.

Heretofore, J.T.'s history had no references to the feelings that swept over him once Daisy was in his presents, he just wasn't aware that the emotion he felt was approaching the caring for a woman. When he neared her camp site she was busy putting all of Stepp's clothes to one side figuring that there was no sentimental value from her point of view and beside less weight in the wagon made for an easier pull for the team. For Daisy there was no need for tears her man was a burden that would not be missed. "Good day Miss Daisy," said J.T. in as steady a voice as possible in his condition. Daisy looked up from her task with a full smile for she recognized the voice of the man who had been so helpful through the circumstances of her husbands shooting.

"So glad to see you again, I figured you to be out looking for a spot to forge the stream this early." Said Daisy. Her words indicating her admiration of J.T. Others in the camp had spoken of his and Targets talents of the land ahead during the gossip in the early evening after cooking time.

"Miss Daisy, I thought it best to stop to let you understand my want to say how sorry I am about what happened here at that card game," J.T. said, with a strong note of genuine sympathy. "The short trip up stream to visit Garth and Brie caused me to see you as a real friend."

Daisy moved closer to make an important point to this man that she was sure spoke straight and would want her to do the same.

"Mr. J.T. between you and me and that white beach tree over there, there is no loss in my heart for that man, the only gift that came from him in the last three years is that boy sitting over there who looks up to you so soon after Mr. Stepp's death. He does so simply because of your kindness to him the on that day, A kindness that was missing with his father. I'll go further with this confession. I have a strong feeling you understand me and life out here in the wilderness which can be all to short. Getting flat-out to the point seems to me to be the best path to take."

J.T. taken back some, kept his head and simply asked her if he might stay the morning and help her get things together. His kindness is what she accepted and so began their friendship. J.T. did ask her at one point if she would like to take a ride to the ridge above camp to see the view overlooking the bend in the river below. Daisy ask him to put his suggestion off for a few days, but did refuse with a warm smile looking at him directly. The wagon was in the best condition, Stepp had taken care of each detail from canvas cover to grease in all wheels. The three horses were also well groomed thanks to Daisy and her way with animals.

Target rode up to the wagon at noon after having crossed the river to look at it's level and to confirm his choice of spot to take the train across. He was welcomed by Daisy and asked to set off his horse for a cup of coffee she had over to low fire. He readily accepted as much for the drink as to see how his friend J.T. was handling himself with his new lady friend.

Targets news was that the crossing should be happening within the next few days. Target was to ask for a meeting of the wagon train master to share his advice on the move. His idea was to send a few wagons over as soon as possible to set up a camp on the other side to best facilitate as smooth a crossing as possible- he would also suggest using ropes if needed and allowing a catch area downstream for any people or animals that could be swept away in the fast moving water. Daisy was impressed with his knowledge and foresight and as he spoke Daisy's son Jed crawled up into J.T.'s lap to better listen to the men's tales.

The first wagon to attempt to cross the river left the camp the next morning after a heated discussion between those that wanted to wait and those that felt that it was best to move on. At the meeting of the wagon master and the few men chosen to lead the crossing Target did put forth many of the better suggestions.

Target volunteered to take the first team and wagon across, he had already brought a team of four draft stallions to the other side to help with a tow line if needed. The wagon chosen, with her permission, given only if she could join the crossing was Daisy's.

J.T. took the reins and eased the team into the water the wagon was filled to capacity to weigh in down to prevent it's flouting. At mid stream the team's hoofs left firm bed and began a swimming motion the wagon holding fast unable to continue it's forward motion without the true pull of the horses. At a red flag motion from Target the team of four on the west bank were put into action pulling the wagon with a rope that got the team to some sure footing and then completed the crossing to the cheers of the crowd gathered on the east bank. Daisy jumped from the rear of the wagon to wave at her son on the other side then moved to the front of the wagon to give J.T. a hug that he had never, in his life time, received from a woman. A affectionate hug that was delivered with a warmth meant to signal this man that he should stay close today tomorrow and forever.

Target the ever romantic breathed a sigh, in his heart he was sure two of his companions were in the ring of romance that would create long term relationships. Once every last wagon and family with all their animals were across they would continue west to the big water.

20

Meeting and Moving on

The wagon train must be left behind for it advanced in miles far too few for Target, Garth and J.T. They were accustomed to moving at a pace that would be at least twice as fast as the train. Target had Daisy placed her wagon at the edge of camp. His reason, he told her was to have a meeting of minds, to put aside any coyness and settle what could be lost if decisions were delayed. She agreed, "Nothing is to be written in stone, lets just put chips on the table and see who bets," said Daisy.

She felt J.T. was her man even though she hadn't been able to get him to even sit close to her, he would need teaching. He would need to be coaxed into her arms and she was the woman to do just that, willingly!

"So what's the big meeting about?" Asked Garth as he, Brie, and J.T. walked in step across the large circle within the wagons. Garth and Brie were fully aware what was to happen but kept still as Target had asked them to. Many looked up from their camp fires to holler out their thanks to these men who successfully helped to get them across the river without any loss of property or life.

"Can't say as I can give out any clues as to what's up," said J.T. as they approached Daisy's wagon where Target sat with little Jed in his lap. Daisy was at work on the nights dinner, brought to her earlier by J.T. who had then rode out to do some hunting.

"Some food will be ready shortly if anyone would sit awhile," said Daisy.

Target spoke next asking all to sit close up to he and Jed so as he wouldn't be including all of the neighbor's in what ideas he had to share with them.

"The way I see it," he began, "is that this group of individuals sitting here are as strong a group of characters as anyone could meet. I can't believe that we should split up tomorrow morning or any morning in the future. I believe that as a tight unit we could break away from the wagon train and double our miles each day with our own freedom of movement. We have the best animals, a strong wagon, a similar destination, and a mutual admiration for each other."

Before anyone had a chance to add a comment Daisy spoke looking directly at J.T. and said, "J.T., I would consider it an honor if you were to join Jed and I in following Target, Brie, and Garth to San Francisco. You are a man I think highly of and hope that you will accept me as your close companion."

J.T. stood and moved to Daisy without a word he took her in his arms and kissed her well on the mouth - no more had to be said. The bantam travel group of, Targets Own, had been created.

Daisy whispered into J.T.'s ear that she would ride up to see the view he had asked her to see anytime. All is well in the world thought J.T.

Christopher carefully returns the leather bound manuscript to it's original resting place on the desk in Garth's just-rented old room. He had been totally absorbed in this tale written by Garth's grandfather Target for what seemed like only minutes when the land lady tapped on the door to see if all was as it should be. "I'm so sorry," said Christopher, my mind has been captured by a story told by Garth's grandfather and all time was put aside. I shall return with the rent balance tomorrow morning and ask that you please not move anything from Garth's room as I shall take it as is." "That will be fine," said the landlady pleased that she had no work ahead - moving items out to the street for pick up. His hope was to finish reading the entire manuscript once he had settled in.

List of future Chapter's

—m—

- High Heel and his effort to retrieve the Winchester
- Captain Mac, a heated reunion
- Target and his struggle with race hate
- Upjohn appears once again
- Time or two in towns along the trail
- Horse race 20 miles through trails - large purse
- Target meets a native Indian woman
- San Francisco the Future

Acknowledgments

The word processing software used in writing this first installment of my triptic was Nisus Writer Pro.